Hot Shot

Hot as Puck

Book Two

Rhian Cahill

Hot Shot
Hot as Puck Book Two
By Rhian Cahill

For more information visit:
www.rhiancahill.com

For Mr.C
Together forever.

PUCK BUNNY PROMOTIONS

UP TO DATE BUNNY TO WIFE ANNOUNCEMENTS

Puck bunnies all over the country are crying themselves to sleep tonight as another pair of eligible skates has left the ice.

We have it from reliable sources that another puck bunny has been promoted. Celeste Dupree has been linked with several players over the years, but it seems she's made her final choice and snagged herself the New York Knights hot shot Branton Lattimer.

Pictures shared with us show a beaming bride, and the smile on Celeste's face clearly shows she's thrilled to be on the arm of her man.

We here at Puck Bunny Promotions have to admit we're shocked by the union. We didn't see this one coming. And from what we hear, neither did anyone else.

And it seems the new Mr. & Mrs. Lattimer aren't just celebrating their nuptials. We're told by our sources that they're expecting the arrival of Baby Lattimer in early spring.

Guess our happy couple didn't wait for their wedding night.

OFF THE ICE

INSIDE THE LIVES OF YOUR FAVORITE NHL PLAYERS

In what's being called a tragic accident, New York Knights right winger, Branton Lattimer, has lost his wife and newborn daughter.

Details are sketchy, but our sources say the pair were involved in some kind of fall at the family home resulting in multiple injuries for both.

We were unable to get comment from either Lattimer or his agent, nor the Knights org.

We'll be sure to update you as more information becomes available on this devastating event.

BLAKE

"Are you sure about this?"

My eyes focus on Dad. "Yes."

"Still think you're an idiot," Landon mutters.

"Nobody asked for your opinion, Landon."

My brother visibly cringes at the sound of Mom's voice. She isn't on the screen, hasn't shown her face on this video call with the men I respect most when it comes to hockey, but I knew she wouldn't be far away.

She never is from Dad, or he her. They say it's because they spent so much time apart when he played in the NHL and the years coaching after that.

"If you're sure, then tell me what you need."

Dad's question has my gaze moving from my brother back to him. Despite this being a video call with six people on the screen, I know my dad is looking right at me, his eyes boring into mine, hunting for any weakness or uncertainty.

I also see trust, pride, and a little concern. All of it stems from his knowledge of me. He knows.

Knows I wouldn't go into this without one hundred percent confidence in my ability to achieve my objective.

Knows if I wasn't sure, I wouldn't willingly put myself in a position to be hurt again.

Knows that's exactly what I'm doing.

Branton Lattimer has the power to hurt me.

Hell, he already has.

But none of that matters. It's in the past, and now, in the present, I'm all about building a future.

And that future means I have to face the one man I swore I wouldn't get close to again.

Not that he's shown any sign of letting either of us be close. He's done everything in his power to push me out of his life—everyone he used to be close to out of his life.

Sighing, I rub a hand on my forehead and think about what it is I need from Dad right now.

Nothing comes to mind.

Hell, I don't even know if Bran will talk to me, never mind listen to our offer.

"I'm good for now. We're flying out tomorrow to go see him."

"We?" Sutton asks.

My eyes flick to my older brother; he's been quiet until now. Our oldest brother, Mason, has been tightlipped as well and I wonder if it's because they don't approve of my decision to be the one from the Rogues org to talk to Bran. I can put their minds at ease if it is.

"Yeah, *we*. Oakley, Walker, and me."

"I assume you're referring to Walker Alcott, Oakley's fiancé," Dad asks.

"Husband."

"What?"

"Since when?"

"What the hell?"

I laugh at the boys' reactions. It breaks the tension, and my body relaxes as I lean back in my chair. "They got married a couple of days ago. Just them, Oakley's Pa, and Micky, the little boy Walker's cousin left him guardian of."

"I heard about that." Mom's face crowds out Dad's, her concern clearly etched around her eyes, in her gaze, in the lopsided frown I remember from my childhood. "Is he okay? Micky? Does he need anything? Do they need anything? You tell Oakley to call me if they need help. Walker too. For anything at all."

I smile at her. "I will." Mom hums as if she knows neither of them is likely to reach out before moving out of frame again. "I promise I'll pass on your message and remind them regularly," I reassure in the hope of appeasing her.

Although I won't be surprised if she sends a care package or even turns up, my dad in tow, to offer her help in person. She's loved Oakley like a second daughter since she and I became unlikely best friends when we were young.

"Is Alcott going as Oakley's husband or…"

Rolling my lips between my teeth, I'm the one keeping quiet now. I hope Sutton lets the question drop.

There's been speculation in the press, but the Rogues org hasn't made an official announcement about Walker's employment as head coach.

Hell, there's still chatter about his injuries and retirement. And his relationship with Oakley.

"Right. Well, when are you heading up this way?" Dad asks, clearly knowing I won't be saying a word on the subject of Walker. "Any chance you can squeeze in a quick visit to your old man?"

It'll be more than a quick visit if we—*I*—can convince

Bran to sign with the Rogues but I don't want to jinx anything by making plans yet. "Can I let you know?"

"Of course. The door is always open," Mom says, her head slipping into frame beside Dad's again.

"Okay, thanks." Over the top of my monitor, I see Oakley appear in the doorway of my office; she taps her wrist reminding me we need to get moving, before disappearing. "All right, I gotta go."

After a chorus of goodbyes from my brothers, and an I love you from both my parents, I'm left staring at Mason. He's my oldest brother and he's taken that title seriously my whole life. He hasn't been a second father but at times he's skated close to that line.

"You were quiet," I say, hoping he wasn't that way so he could blast me about my choices now.

"Are you sure?"

"I said I was, didn't I?"

"Yes, but you've never let Dad see your fears. Those you reserved for me or Mom."

True. But then being the only girl in the middle of a pack of boys—and yes, I refer to my brothers as a pack—in a hockey family, fear is something I've strived to hide. "Fear is a healthy motivator."

"It's also a crippling emotion and a survival instinct and—"

"Okay, okay." I hold up a hand. "I get it."

"Well? Are you sure?"

"Yes."

"Is that from a coach's perspective or a girlfriend's?"

"We never dated." Not for lack of wanting on either side. Or at least I didn't believe it was one sided.

"No? Then what would you call what you two were?"

A sigh slips free, and I rub my forehead again. "I don't know. Best friends?"

"And yet you heard he was married through the media?"

"Mason. No one knew he was marrying her until it broke on *Puck Bunny Promotions*." Fuck, I hate that blog.

"Fine." He holds up both hands. "I'll leave it alone. For now."

"Thank you."

"Don't thank me yet. If he hurts you like that again, I'll cut his balls off."

"You don't think he's suffered enough?"

My brother's face scrunches with pain and sorrow and regret. "No one should suffer like that."

"Agreed. Now I really have to go. Give my love to Cash when you see him."

"Will do. Call me after you get things sorted with Branton. I've got a lead on a goalie for you. If you're interested."

I straighten, my interest definitely engaged. "Yeah?"

"He's young, or he was, he'd be twenty-one now, still young I guess. I don't know the full story yet but I'm getting it because I've seen him on the ice. Then and now."

"Give me his name, his details? I'll get Nat to look into him."

"Not yet. Get this thing with Branton squared away first."

Scowling at my brother, I hope my death glare will change his mind but all I get is a laugh followed by I love you before he disappears from my screen leaving mine the only face left.

I can't stop the growl of frustration dealing with my family has rumbling in my chest.

"Mason has a goalie for us?"

I look up to find Nat standing in my doorway, Oakley behind her. Nodding I say, "Not that he's sharing."

"Hmm…" Nat doesn't say anything else. But the frown on her face tells me my brother will be receiving a call from her in the near future. She's not one to sit around and wait and I have to grin at the thought of how that call might go. Oh, to be a fly on the wall...

"C'mon, let's go," Oakley says. "Walker and Micky are waiting with their gear to check out the practice rink."

Pushing back my chair, I stand and move around my desk. Scooping up my own bag of gear and slipping it over my shoulder, I make my way over to them and bring up the elephant in the room. "Cami coming?"

Nat scoffs like I'm an idiot for asking and Oakley laughs, though there's no humor in it.

"Right. That's a no."

Oakley shrugs. She's getting better at letting Cami keep her distance. I understand why she wants her here—involved with the Rogues—and I understand why Cami doesn't want to be.

She'll come around, I know she will. Once the team is here, once we start playing in the league. I'd put my gold medals down on the fact she'll be as deeply entangled in the Rogues as the rest of us once the arena is finished and the staff and players start wandering the corridors, skating on the ice. Speaking of...

I slip my arm through Oakley's, drag her to catch up to Nat and loop my other arm through hers. "This is it, ladies, every-thing we've been working toward is right at our fingertips."

"Not everything yet, but we're close." Rolling my eyes at Nat, I poke my tongue out at her. "Oh, very mature."

"Stop raining on my parade," I say.

"I'm being realistic."

I halt our movement, yanking them both back a little as I do. "I'll give you realistic. We own a hockey team. In the *national* league. The *men's* league."

Smiles curve both their mouths.

"Damn straight we do."

Spinning around, our arms and feet get tangled and when

the three of us finally right ourselves I don't know which one of us is more shocked.

"You came." Oakley's words are filled with disbelief, but her face shows the relief the sight of our fourth partner delivers.

"We get to see the finished practice rink today, right?" There's a little insecurity in Cami's voice and I launch forward and pull her into a hug.

"Yes! We do. It's the first piece other than the original apartment block and these offices we can actually use. I'm so excited to get out there and see how it feels under my blades." Letting go, I link our arms and turn to the others. "All right, ladies, let's go see what four kick-ass women have achieved."

BRANTON

"Laura!"

I'm on the lake.

"Laura!"

It's always the lake.

I know I shouldn't be out here but I'm chasing Laura. She's just up ahead and I know it's not safe.

"Laura!"

Neither of us should be here. It's thin ice I'm skating on and it won't hold my weight for long but every time I reach out, my fingertips barely brush Laura's clothes before she pulls away again.

"Laura!"

It's always the same. No matter how fast I skate, how hard I push, it's never enough.

"Laura!" My shout comes out more of a whisper. The sound raw and raspy. My voice hoarse from calling her name over and over.

It's always like this too, she never stops, is always *just* out of reach.

I need to push harder, get closer but my thighs ache, my muscles screaming from exertion.

My right leg gives under me, my foot breaking through...

Crashing through the ice into the cold water shocks the shit out of me and yanks me from the nightmare, except the water dripping off my head and running down my back is all too real and not a figment of my subconscious mind.

"Jesus fucking Christ!" I swipe a hand over my face and blink at the woman standing in front of me. "Who the hell are you?"

"Your savior or your worst nightmare."

"Huh?" Am I still asleep? Still dreaming? Drops of water fly around as I shake my head in an effort to clear my confusion —or wake my damn ass up! "What?" The word comes out a croak, pain lashing my ravaged throat.

"Your savior or your worst nightmare. You choose."

I don't have time to make sense of her words before Walker Alcott, the captain of my hockey team—no, no longer mine— stands beside her.

"Bran."

"Cap? What the hell?" I have to be asleep. There's no way he's here. In Gannon's house...

"When did you eat last?" Walker asks, his hand stretched out toward me.

"Eh... Dunno." My mind still in a fog from the nightmare, I reach out, grip his hand for a quick shake. He feels real enough, but then all my nightmares are life-like. "What time is it?" I ask, my voice still a rough grumble.

"Almost midday."

My gaze swings back to the woman who's still a mystery. "What day?"

She sucks in a breath, and I can tell she's not happy about

the way this conversation is going. Or maybe it's the subject. My obvious confusion.

Good for her. I don't want to be having this conversation either. Or have either of them here in my living nightmare, my personal banishment.

With a clenched jaw she grinds out, "Thursday."

"Huh." I glance around the room, my eyes landing on the coffee table, the upright bottle in the middle of it. "Not even a bottle," I mutter.

So much for wiping my mind clean and missing today all together.

"How are you doing, Bran?" Walker asks, concern lacing his words, and I look up to find him staring at the bottle of scotch with its inch of amber liquid in the bottom.

I have to laugh. They think I'm a drunk. Fair, considering. Still...

"You think I'm drunk all the time?" I shake my head as I pull my shirt off and slap my abs. "Do these look like I live on alcohol?"

Walker smiles at me and for some reason I want to punch it right off his face even though he appears pleased by my declaration.

"Wanna put those to good use?" he asks.

I raise an eyebrow and shove down the anger boiling to the surface. "Doing?"

"Playing."

"Ha! Like any team is going to want me after what I did." I hate what I did. Would take it back—all of it—if I could.

"The Rogues want you." The woman's words are like a whip, snapping at me and yanking my attention back to her. "We need someone with your skills and experience to guide us to the finals."

"Who the hell are the Rogues?" This conversation is getting more confusing by the second.

Fuck. I must still be asleep. Maybe the scotch I drank in the hope of wiping my memory—of avoiding today—is giving me weird dreams. Hallucinations. Nightmares.

No, the nightmares are of my own making.

"The new national league franchise." Walker claps me on the shoulder. "I want you on my team."

"You're playing for them? When did you leave New York?" I don't keep up with the world outside of my self-imposed exile and I don't know what shocks me more, Walker leaving the Knights—where he's been his entire NHL career—for another team or him standing in my living room.

"When Blanchett slammed me into the boards and left me unable to play at a professional level."

"Wait. You're not playing? Then how the hell would I be on your team?"

"I'm coaching. Head coach."

Head coach? *Holy shit!* Walker Alcott is coaching an NHL team? From what he says, a brand spanking new team who wants me...

I look at the woman beside my old captain. "And who the hell are you? The general manager?"

"No. That's Natalie Redding. I'm the team owner and this"—she waves a hand behind me—"is our assistant coach, Blake Watts."

I spin so fast I stumble, air rushing from my lungs as my heart jerks in my chest, slams against my ribcage. "*Blake.*" Her name is an agonized groan as it leaves my throat.

My gaze locks with hers and I lose myself in her quicksilver eyes, every emotion, every thought, every memory comes rushing, an avalanche of sensation I struggle to hold in.

"I..." My body moves a step without thought. "*Blake.*" Her

name is a plea on my tongue, the weight of all that I'm feeling coating each letter. Weighing them down with regret—with longing.

"Bran."

Her voice...

My name...

The sight of her...

It's too much.

All of it.

Everything from the last few years bursts through my muscles and sends me across the room. I have her in my arms. My face pressed against the cool skin of her neck. And for the first time in years, my anguish and sorrow flow out of me.

I have no control, no hope of stopping the flood of emotion pouring out as I pull her harder against me. Hold her tighter than I should.

She's murmuring in my ear, I can't make out a single word, but it doesn't matter. Nothing matters but the comfort of her arms and the sound of her voice, the heat of her body and the scent of her skin.

I have no idea how long I stand there sobbing into her neck, no idea why the sight of her broke through the barriers I've held in place for so long. Too long.

After months and months and months of feeling alone, of feeling raw and wild, the chaos that my life has been settles.

It settles in a way I don't understand. In a way I know can only be a brief reprieve. But I'll take it.

I'll take this moment and breathe it in, take the comfort and care I've been holding at arm's length since the day my life changed, since the moment my whole world fell apart.

I don't know how she does it, but I find myself in my bedroom, being lowered to my bed. The sheets are still rumpled from where I crawled out of them late last night—the early hours of this morning—in search of the oblivion sleep can't bring me.

"I'll be right back."

Her words have me reaching out, my hands grasping, grabbing her shirt and gripping tight. "Don't go." I can hear the desperation in my voice, but it guts me to think of her leaving.

She can't leave me too.

"I'm not leaving, Bran. I just need to tell Oakley and Walker I'm staying with you so they can go."

I nod my head as her hand sweeps over my hair, urges me down on the pillow. "Okay."

"Lie back down. Close your eyes, go to sleep. Just rest if you can't. I'll be here when you get up, Bran."

I don't know if it's her touch or her words—the conviction in them—that has me closing my eyes and slipping into that drowsy space between consciousness and sleep.

I listen to her breathe, feel the heat of her next to me.

She's here. Finally here after all this time and everyone else I love is gone.

The last thing I register is the scent of her in my nose and the warmth of her hand against my skin.

BLAKE

When I reach the bedroom door I glance over my shoulder at a slumbering Bran and wonder how long it will last.

If I read him right, as well as the evidence in the living room, he hasn't consumed more than three quarters of a bottle. Not enough to be worried about unless we're talking hangovers.

Finding the house empty, I head to the front door and see Oakley and Walker in the driveway. I assume she's pumping Walker for any information he might know about my relationship with Bran.

Years ago, I kept her, Nat, and Cami in the dark about how close Bran and I had gotten. And when he got married, I saw no reason to enlighten them.

Especially when I knew they'd only worry about me and in all likelihood, smother me in their love and concern. Not that there's anything wrong with that but at the time I wasn't ready to expose the wounds Bran getting married had given me.

When the news he'd snuck off and married Celeste—that

they were expecting a baby—had broken, I'd been more confused than angry. Although anger should have won out.

He'd gone and done the very things that had kept us from crossing the line of friendship to lovers.

The things neither of us had wanted *yet*.

The things we'd talked about having in the future— *together*.

Giving myself a mental slap, I pull myself out of my head and focus on now. "Oakley."

Two sets of concerned eyes turn toward me but it's Oakley who speaks.

"Yeah."

Her gaze bores into mine like she can read my mind, like if she looks hard enough she can find the answers to the questions I know she has.

"I'm staying. Give me a few days and I'll let you know if we need to keep looking or if Bran is joining us."

"You're staying here?"

I see her concern, those questions that must be burning her tongue, but I can't take the time to explain. "For now."

"Should I worry about you? What that was about?"

Shaking my head, I give her a small smile. "No. We're good. I'm good."

"I don't want to leave if—"

"I'll be fine. Bran isn't who the media made him out to be." I know I'm going on past behavior, that him up and marrying Celeste and shutting me out proved what I knew to be a lie, but I didn't accept it then, I can't accept now. I've known him for years, since the scrawny six-year-old turned up at our house and began training with my dad like the rest of us.

"No one ever is," Oakley says, pulling in a deep breath. If anyone knows about the bullshit often printed in the media, it's her. "Okay, keep me posted. If I don't hear from you in... three days, I'm coming back."

"You won't have to. Promise." I won't need to worry about her coming back at that deadline. I'll be in touch before that, and I'm determined to be at my parents' place—with Bran—by then anyway.

Coming up the steps she pulls me into a tight hug and whispers, "Call for anything, doesn't have to be about the Rogues."

"Thanks. Safe trip home." When I pull away, I wave to Walker and call out, "See you later, Cap."

"Cap?" Oakley asks.

I'm smiling now. My first real smile since we found Bran on the floor and my heart dropped from my chest to join him. "It's what Bran called him. I forgot he was captain of the Knights. See you both later."

I slip back inside and close the door. I know they have questions, especially Oakley, and probably want to stick around and help, but this needs to be only me and Bran for now. We need to know—okay, *I* need to know—that we can pull some of the remnants of our previous friendship together before either of us can decide if we're able to work together, and we can't do that with others around.

A quick check on Bran shows he's still sleeping in what appears to be peaceful slumber, although I'm not sure anyone who's been through what he has can ever find peace.

Leaving him to his post-breakdown nap, I close the bedroom door except for a few inches, and explore the rest of the house.

There's one more bedroom, barely big enough for the bed in it but at least it's not a twin. A small functional bathroom across the hall has no wet towels or toiletries so I assume there's a second one off Bran's room. The living room and dining are one space with the wall that faces the trees behind the house made up of windows.

From out front, the house looks rundown and possibly inhabitable, but inside...

Inside is a revelation.

Gannon Byrd must have fixed the place up for his grandmother after he made the NHL. As I look around, I see little touches that wouldn't have come from him or Bran. They have to be left over from the woman who lived in this house her entire life, raised Gannon in from the time he was four.

Heading for the kitchen, I grab a roll of paper towels and go back to clean up the mess Oakley made.

I can't say I agree with her method, but she certainly got Bran's attention.

Something I haven't been able to do in years.

Maybe now, with both of us stuck here, he'll have to talk to me. Have to let me in.

The crushing embrace he gave me before he broke down says there's a crack in his armor that wasn't there before. And all I need is a thin break, just enough to wiggle in and find my old friend.

I'd ignored Corbin's and Landon's words when they told me he wasn't the same man, now and when he'd first cut me out of his life. I understood the need to change our friendship after he had a wife but the complete severing of it in such an abrupt way didn't seem like Bran at all.

I hate to point fingers and I know I hold a small amount of jealousy toward Celeste, but how could I not?

She got what we'd talked about. What we'd decided to wait for.

God! I let him talk me into waiting until—

"Blake?"

The anguished cry has me dropping the roll of towels and running in the direction of the bedrooms only to collide with Bran as he bursts into the hall. Bouncing off his hard chest, I crash into the wall and would have landed on the floor if he didn't have lightning quick, hockey-honed reflexes.

"Sorry."

"Not your fault. I was rushing." Something I need to put a stop to. I might want him for the team, might want to try to rekindle our friendship, but I can't let myself be consumed by him and his needs no matter how much I want to make him feel better.

"I thought you were a dream." His hands tighten on my upper arms, his eyes searching mine. "Are you really assistant coach for the new NHL team?"

"Baton Rouge Rogues. We're the Rogues."

The grin he gives me does crazy things to my belly. It's swooping and twisting and I know I'm fucked.

There's no way I can stop my old feelings from resurfacing —for the hurts that have festered for years from oozing out to taint what is now.

"The Rogues, huh? So what, Walker is Captain Rogue?"

"Oh my god! That's it!" Pulling from his grip I race back to where I left my bag. Searching inside, I grab my phone and fire off a quick text to the girls.

Team mascot. Captain Rogue. Pirate.

NAT

Love it!

OAKLEY

That fits perfectly!

CAMI

Good job, Blake.

Wasn't me. Bran came up with it. I'll explain later. Gotta get back to securing our hot shot.

"I've missed that smile."

Bran's voice has my head snapping up. His words may say he's happy to see me but the frown on his face doesn't. "That's not a good thing?"

"What? No. Missing you is not a good thing. It's horrible. Gut scraping."

"Then why wouldn't you answer my calls? Why did you cut me off—" I throw up a hand. "You know what, I don't want to get into that right now. I haven't eaten since the plane. What have you got in the way of food?"

I don't give him a chance to argue when I brush past him and head for the kitchen. Seeing him again is dragging up things I thought I'd be okay handling. Except I don't think I am. And while I still think securing him for the team is the right thing, I'm rethinking my idea that I'm the right person to convince him.

"If the offer is real, I'll take it."

I spin around to find Bran right behind me.

So close.

Too close.

Taking a step back, my butt bumps up against the kitchen counter. "What?"

"If the offer to play for the team, the Rogues, is real. I'll take it. Do you have a contract here?"

"Don't you want to know the deal? Talk it over with your agent?"

"He dropped me."

"Oh."

"Are you the assistant coach. Is Walker head?"

I nod. "Yes, to both."

"Then it's three yeses. I want on your team. When do we start?"

"Bran, you should…" What am I doing? Am I going to talk him out of what we want? "Before you agree, I've got a condition. I want to head home and do some training with you."

"No."

"Why not?"

"We stay here. For the next week. We stay here and clear the stuff between us before we go anywhere else."

"And if I say no to doing that?" Is he trying to blackmail me with his agreement to join the Rogues?

"I'll sign a contract after you give me the week." He steps closer and everything in me wants to retreat but I've got nowhere to go.

"Bran."

"*Please*. Give me the week." He swallows hard, rakes a hand through his hair. "It'll take me that long to explain everything."

"I don't need to know—"

"You do. Most might not, but *you*, yeah, you deserve to know. You deserve everything and once I've explained things, if you can still bear to look at me, I'll join your team and play the hardest I've ever played. I'll do it for you because I owe you."

"You owe me noth—"

"Everything. I owe you everything."

BRANTON

"Let's eat. Food first. Make decisions on staying after." I move around her and open the fridge. "I've got leftover lasagna or beef stew."

"Is the stew your mom's recipe?"

"Would it be anything else?" I glance over my shoulder to see her smiling. I could stare at that smile all day.

Fuck, I have stared at it all day. Often enough for it to be etched in my memory. It's that memory above all others I couldn't bring myself to think about since everything went to shit because I know I took it away from her.

I didn't witness it, the sadness my actions caused her, because I'm a coward and had no idea how to explain Celeste, but I knew about it.

Her brothers, two of my closest friends before my life took a detour, made sure I knew about the stripping of Blake's smile. About the sadness and hurt I inflicted.

"Bran?"

"What? Sorry. Stew, right?" I force a smile, the action stiff and foreign but I hope it's enough to derail any questions. I meant what I said, I want to enjoy a meal with her before we tackle anything else, before I confess the mistakes I made.

"Yes, I can never pass up the opportunity to have your mom's food, especially her stew." Her smile is sad this time. Like me, she's probably remembering the woman whose love language was feeding you, a language she excelled at.

"I'm sure mine isn't the same, isn't as good, but it comes close." Turning back to the fridge I grab the container of stew and move to the stove where I pour the fragrant beef mixture into a saucepan and light the burner. "How hungry are you? There's probably just enough for two if you're not starving."

"Got some bread to go with it?"

"Yeah, the loaf of sourdough I made two days ago should still be okay, we can toast it if it's gone stale. It's in the cupboard over there." I indicate the one I'm talking about with a chin lift. It's vague but with our history Blake knows exactly which one I'm pointing at.

The reminder of how well we know each other, how in sync we are—*were*—is one more slash of the emotional knife to my heart. I should never have left her out of what was happening, should never have cut her from my life no matter how disgusted with myself I was, no matter how much I hated what I'd done.

She would have forgiven me the first mistake, would have helped me find a different way—

"Do you want to eat inside or out on the deck?"

"Out. We can turn on the heaters to keep us warm."

I love being outside. The only thing stopping me from moving out there is the wall of windows in the living room. They make it feel like you're outside when you're in.

I've spent most of my time since I came up here in that room or out on the deck. Driven there when my mind replays the past on a loop in my head.

"Drink?"

"I'm good with water."

"Not cold?" She sends me a smirk and I'm a little flummoxed as to why until I remember the drenching I received from Oakley James. How I didn't recognize Blake's best friend is a mystery. Although I haven't seen her in years, she was once a regular visitor to the Watts house.

"She's still a firecracker."

Blake laughs and I close my eyes, absorbing the sound. "Yeah. Not much has changed with Oakley."

"What made her decide to go after an NHL franchise?" I ask just as the stew begins to bubble. "Wait, don't answer that yet. Grab a couple of bowls for me to scoop this into. If you carry the drinks out, I'll bring the food."

Again, Blake follows my chin lift in the right direction and finds the bowls instantly. Two appear beside me before she fills glasses with water from the tap and heads for the sliding door to the deck.

It only takes me a few minutes to dish out the stew, grab a couple of spoons, and follow. I take a second to flick the switch to light four of the outdoor heaters Gannon had fitted for his grandmother who loved to sit outside on snowy winter nights. It's the reason one wall of the living room is all windows too. So she could easily see those nights when going outside was impossible.

Placing one bowl in front of Blake, I take the seat next to her instead of the one across where she set my drink.

I might have put distance between us in recent years but now that she's here, I can't keep that up. Can't deny I want to get as close to her as she'll let me. I use my spoon to point at her bowl. "Eat, then answer my question about the team."

She doesn't object to the command, and that's how it came out with the way my voice is gravelly from lack of sleep and use

—more of the latter. She digs right into the hearty meal and the sound she makes when the first spoonful passes her lips has my body reacting.

It's a reaction I need to shut down.

I've wanted Blake Watts for as long as I've known what wanting means, *fuck*, before I knew what it meant, and yet I never allowed myself to have her. I can't explain why, all I know is I didn't want to complicate our friendship—our bond—with sex. Not then.

And look where that got me. Maybe if I had let us get physical, I wouldn't have found myself in the situation that almost destroyed me.

Fuck. It might still destroy me.

I push my seat back. "We forgot the bread." I need a moment to get my body and mind under control. I've never had an issue doing either before, but I can feel the fine layer of desperation lacing the lust coursing through me and I know I need to get away or I'll do something stupid.

Like kiss her.

Taking my time—not too much or our food will go cold—I slice four pieces and head back outside.

"Thanks." She takes a slice and dips it into her bowl before I've lowered the plate all the way to the table. After several bites she breaks the rest up and drops it on top of the stew. I have to remind myself to stop watching her and eat my own food.

I'm halfway through my second piece of bread when she breaks the silence.

"*We* went after it."

"What?"

"The NHL franchise. *We* went after it."

"We?"

"Me, Oakley, Cami, and Nat."

"I get Oakley, but Cami and Nat... Wait. Aren't they

Rogue sportswear... which is owned by KAW.... KAW owns the franchise. And KAW is the four of you." I speak as my mind works to connects the dots.

"Still not just a pretty face," she says with a grin.

"Not even that without my teeth in." I grin back showing off the pearly whites a dentist provided.

"Teeth or not, your face is still pretty, Bran."

I don't want her to go down the attraction road. We need to work out the crap scattered over the road of our friendship first and I doubt she'll ever see me as pretty again once she knows the truth. "So KAW got the franchise. When did that happen?"

"We signed the contract with the league a few weeks ago. It wasn't meant to be announced until the end of the month but someone leaked info about the deal almost immediately after we signed, so we had a rushed press conference in New York to make the announcement."

"And how did it go over? The new team being in Baton Rouge? That's where you said it was located, right?"

"Yes. We decided to use Oakley and Cami's hometown because the new headquarters and manufacturing facility for Rogue sportswear is being built there and we want the two businesses to complement each other."

"Bring people into the area to work on the sportswear, give them something to do in their spare time."

"That's kind of basic, but yes. The two KAW companies will share some facilities like childcare centers, food and beverage outlets, and a small shopping mall with a grocery store. There's also two housing developments in the works plus the one we already completed in preparation for when the first employees begin working at the head office or the arena now the announcement has been made."

"Sounds like you're building a mini city."

With a shrug, she says, "I guess, in some ways we are. But it's more about community. We want the Rogues team to be a family like we've done with the sportswear brand and for both to mesh. We want the place we locate both to benefit from them as well. For that to be a success, we need to be sure we're giving our employees—all of them—and the people already living in Baton Rouge what they deserve. Treat them well and they'll be happy and stick around."

"If I remember right, getting a job at Rogue sportswear is like finding a needle in a haystack."

"Still is."

"So the idea behind getting an NHL franchise?"

"Came from Gerald Cantrell Senior, actually."

"Really?" The previous owner of the Knights was a great man. One who had been extra generous when my life spiraled out of control then went up in a fireball of hell flames.

"Yep. He told Oakley we had the knowledge and skills to do it and it would be a good complement to our sportswear brand so we should look at one of the teams in the national women's league."

"Oh boy." Cantrell Senior had waved a proverbial red flag in front of four women who, in my experience, liked to prove they can do anything.

Blake quickly swallows her last bite of stew. "Oh boy is right. It was an insult without being one, but we liked the idea, took it as a challenge, and here we are."

"Here you are."

Here she is.

Right next to me.

Giving me a sense of stability I haven't felt since the day I woke up to find Celeste Dupree in bed next to me.

BLAKE

Night steals over the surrounding forest, cloaking us in darkness while we talk, and in spite of the outdoor heaters, the cold wraps around us too. We've been out here an hour or so, talking mainly about the new Rogues facility, the practice rink that's already up and running as of yesterday, the gym and change rooms that were due to be cleared for use today.

"Do you like living there? The heat?" Bran asks.

"It's not too bad. Although I am looking forward to spending a lot more time inside the training facility and arena. Both are at temps more to my liking."

"I remember you voting against the trip to Hawaii the year your brothers and I graduated high school and they got to pick the family holiday destination."

"I remember someone else being just as vocal about their choice." I glance around. "And it's not like you found yourself a tropical island to hide out on."

"Who said I'm hiding?"

I bring my gaze back to Bran. Stare at him with disbelief

and disappointment because we never used to lie or twist the truth with each other. "Lie to yourself if you have to but we both know you're in hiding."

He has the grace to blush and drop his gaze. "Sorry. I've gotten used to deflecting—lying—to those closest to me. Not that there are many people left in my inner circle."

"No one but yourself to blame for that. You shoved us all out of it, Bran."

"I did. I know I did." He looks away, out into the darkness and says, "But I had to. I couldn't lie to you all every damn day and if we'd stayed close, if I had let you all stay in my life, I would have had to."

"Why? Why would you have to lie to anyone?"

His gaze moves back to lock with mine, his eyes blazing with anger and resentment—regret. "Because it was all a lie."

"What was?"

"My *marriage*." He spits the second word out like it burns his tongue. "A marriage that should never have happened!"

He shoves his chair back, toppling it over when he surges to his feet. I don't have time to get a word out or rise from my own seat before he's storming into the house. I'm sure if the door to inside was a normal one, he would have slammed it behind him, but the glass slider is too heavy, and it slips quietly into the frame.

I don't know what the hell he's talking about. He married Celeste because of the baby—his child.

My gaze stays glued to the spot I last saw him, my mind spinning with questions.

"Because it was all a lie."

Out of everything he said, those six words run on repeat in my head and the only conclusion I can come to after his outburst is Celeste lied about being pregnant...but the baby was born seven months after the news of their marriage...unless the baby wasn't his.

Oh my god.

Could she have lied about the baby being Bran's?

Why did he stay if that was the case?

And who was the father if not Bran?

Celeste had a reputation for jumping from player to player. It was one of the shocking parts of Bran marrying her. She wasn't his type. At all. He wasn't hers either. She went for the cocky players, the ones who used their celebrity status and partied all the time.

I still don't understand how they got together in the first place. I hadn't been aware of them dating. They hadn't been spotted together before the photo of a stern looking Bran and a grinning Celeste was splashed on the *Puck Bunny Productions* blog, every media outlet in the country picking the story up within hours.

I'm getting ahead of myself. I don't know what he means. It could be Celeste lied about being pregnant then got pregnant after they were married. It could be any number of possibilities.

Shaking my head, I slowly stand and gather our dishes. There's no point trying to figure it out when I don't have all the facts. And I'm not about to go find Bran and ask all the questions burning a path from my brain to my tongue.

Instead I'll clean up after our meal, then call it a night even though it's early. I should check in with Oakley and Nat. Although, if I speak to either of them, they'll know something is bothering me and I don't want to answer their questions right now just as I know Bran doesn't want to answer mine.

Not yet anyway.

Earlier I thought I wasn't prepared for the emotions being

around Bran delivered. Now I don't think I'm ready for the revelations he's going to reveal.

He seemed so angry and hurt and all I wanted to do was soothe him the way I did when his mother died.

Everyone thought I was upset and angry at Bran, that he'd betrayed me, but the biggest sorrow I have is that I couldn't be there for him in his darkest days. That I couldn't help him navigate the turmoil of losing his wife and child.

A wife he seems to hate.

A daughter he hasn't mentioned.

A family there is no evidence ever existed in his life.

Why are there no pictures around? If he was grieving their loss, wouldn't he have something to look at? He did when he lost his mother. Had pictures of her everywhere in his apartment because he was afraid he might forget what she looked like.

There's none of that here.

Dumping our dishes in the sink, I head back outside to work out how to turn off the heaters and lock up the house. It feels a little cold inside; I'll have to find the house's heat source and turn that up. Then again, the coolness might be from us coming in and out.

I find a set of switches labeled deck heaters and turn the ones on off. Securing the sliding glass door, I consider drawing the curtains across it to help warm things up but then I spot the thermostat and see Bran has got it set low.

I have to laugh at myself.

A few years ago, twenty degrees Celsius wouldn't have made me blink but living in the south seems to have thinned my blood.

My brothers and father would have a field day with that. Mom would understand completely though. She was born and raised in Arizona and still complains about the cold of Canada and she's lived here for over thirty years now.

I've got warm clothes and I brought the snuggly flannel pjs Mom got me last Christmas after listening to me complain one too many times about how cold it is getting out of bed in the mornings when I'm home.

I grin when I think about her matching pair and how Dad just rolled his eyes at us while my brothers groaned.

I never go home without them which is why I have them now. I can slip them on and go straight to bed after I clean up from dinner. I still alter the temp on the furnace, turning it up a few degrees.

Five to be exact.

Twenty-five seems far more comfortable than twenty.

When I finish loading the dishwasher and put away the loaf of bread Bran left out, I hunt around to see if I can find the fixings for hot chocolate. I'm not a tea drinker and the last thing I need is coffee right before bed.

I'm not surprised to find what I'm looking for. One of my most cherished memories of Bran's mom is her hot chocolate and the nights she'd made it for us. We'd sit up late and talk, a hot cup, loaded with marshmallows, cradled in our hands.

His mother refused to make it any other way than with real chocolate. She'd buy blocks of it and shave it before stirring it into a pan of warming milk. I found a quicker way that doesn't taste quite as good but it's better than going without.

It seems Bran likes to make it the way his mother did because I find a container of shaved chocolate in the pantry right beside a packet of open marshmallows.

I know I shouldn't, but I head toward the bedrooms. Tap lightly on Bran's door.

I don't expect an answer. I certainly don't expect him to open the door in his underwear.

But one second I'm standing contemplating knocking again and the next I'm staring at a bare chest.

"I'm sorry."

"Ah." The sound hasn't even finished leaving my lips when he's talking again.

"I shouldn't have yelled. Shouldn't have stormed away. Shouldn't have waited until you knocked to apologize."

"Um…" I drag my gaze up to his. "That's a lot of shouldn'ts."

He scrubs a hand over his head and grips the back of his neck. "I keep making mistakes with you. With my life."

"You can't help the way you feel—"

"But I can help the way I treat people no matter how I'm feeling."

I don't want to get into a bash-Bran session so I ask the question I knocked on his door for. "I'm making hot chocolate. Want a cup?"

The smile he gives me is bittersweet and the longing in his eyes has my heart lurching. "Yeah, I'd like that. Want me to light a fire?"

I don't know if we should sit together like we used to. Maybe we should try something different, something that won't bring up the past or have us falling into the discussion I know is inevitable, so I lie. "I was going to take mine to bed. I've got some emails to return."

"Oh. Okay." He looks at his wrist, the one without a watch, and says, "You're right. It is late. And now that I think about it, I'll pass. Do you need anything before I crash?"

"No. I'm good."

"Come get me if you're not."

"Will do." I don't wait for him to close the door in my face. I turn on my heel and head back to the kitchen. I'm no longer in the mood for hot chocolate. I'm not in the mood for anything. Turning off the lights, I grab my bag from near the front door and make my way to the spare bedroom.

Closing the door behind me I take a deep breath and wonder about the unknown wounds Bran has suffered.

Wonder how I'm going to make it through a week of this.

If I'm strong enough to face my wounds where Bran is concerned.

If I'm strong enough to face his.

BRANTON

I watch the sun rise from the front porch. The way the sky changes color and the world around me lightens always brings me a sliver of hope, a few minutes of peace.

Hope for what, I'm not sure, but these quiet early morning minutes have saved me more than once.

The air is frigid, burning through my chest with each breath I take. My nose is numb, my fingers and toes too. I've endured the freezing pre-dawn for thirty minutes, probably should have gone out on to the back deck where I can switch the heaters on to banish the frosty temperature, but the sunrise isn't as good out there.

The peace the breaking morning brings me not as lasting.

It's the shadows of the tall trees surrounding the backyard I think. They keep the light away longer and with it the possibility of a new beginning.

I might be doing something I've done most mornings since I got here. It might seem like nothing has changed. Except everything has.

Blake is here.

And for the first time in months—*years*—I'm thinking about something other than the shit show my life is.

My mind keeps wandering to what it could have been—what it *should* have been.

For as long as I can remember, my future had been clear. Make the professional hockey league and be with Blake.

We'd—*I'd*—stupidly thought we had time. I had it all planned out. I'd hit the league, Blake already deep in her own success with both hockey and her business by then, and we'd both move toward the thing we'd agreed should wait until after we hit our professional goals, until the time was right.

Stupid.

So fucking stupid.

There is no right time.

Life, other people, all move at their own pace and with their own intentions, and those movements trip you up, those intentions detour you, stop you altogether.

I never saw it coming.

The change to my plans—our plans.

Never saw the person who, once her claws were in deep, did everything she could to destroy me, coming.

Thinking back on what I'd done, where I was now, how long I've been in this self-imposed exile, I have to admit she's still destroying me.

How does a dead woman, a woman I hate—will always hate—have the power to ruin me?

So much about my relationship with Celeste was bullshit.

Most of it was bullshit.

Only I hadn't had a clue, had I?

I'd believed her. Believed the story she told.

I didn't understand it, how I'd let it happen, why I'd done it when my heart had been Blake's.

It wasn't until after everything had imploded, after she'd

ruined the one good thing in my life, that I finally understood the lengths Celeste had gone to in a bid to get what she wanted.

And what she wanted wasn't *me*.

It was what I could give her.

Money.

Celebrity.

The trap had been sprung and I'd been oblivious to it. Until the darkest moment of my life when she slapped me in the face with the truth.

A truth my heart still can't believe.

My brain knows it to be true. The science backs that knowledge up, but my heart...

My heart bleeds and aches in a way I'm not sure can ever be repaired.

The door creaks behind me and I brace myself, suck in a deep breath to clear my head of the past and prepare for my future—for the sight of Blake.

"Hey. Why are you out here in the cold?"

"Enjoying the sunrise."

"God, it's cold! Aren't you freezing?"

I am. But it's part of my punishment. Part of the penance I've made myself endure for all the mistakes I made. All the people I hurt. All the things I could have done different and didn't.

"Not too much. Nose, toes, and fingers."

"Jeez. You're not wearing a coat. Fucking hell, Bran, your feet are bare. You'll get frostbite!"

"It's not that bad. I'm used to it."

"You do this every morning?"

"Yes."

"Right. Okay. Well, I'm not freezing my ass off out here. I'm going in to make breakfast. You want something? Coffee?"

"There isn't any."

"What? Food?"

"No. There's food. Eggs and bacon, pancake fixings in the pantry. But there's no coffee."

"You don't have coffee?" she questions, her confusion clear.

I want to laugh but I don't. Coffee is another of life's luxuries I force myself to live without. Although if I'm honest, it was the least difficult to give up. "Haven't so much as sniffed a cup since I left New York."

"Oh."

Funny how that one small word tells me she gets it. "Get inside out of the cold. I'll come in and help you make breakfast when I'm done."

Dammit. I'm dismissing her when I promised myself last night—after our chat at my bedroom door—I'd do my best to not avoid her or the elephant in the room.

"Sorry. I didn't mean that like it sounded," I apologize.

"Didn't you?" She places a hand on my shoulder but remains behind me, my body probably shielding her from the cold breeze. "You're still in defense mode. Protecting your goal. I don't know what happened because you haven't told me, haven't told anyone, but, Bran, I'm not here to hurt you. I'm not here for an explanation or apology. I'm here because I think you'll fit into the Rogues roster and be an integral part of the team, of our success. And because I will always be your friend. You will always be able to rely on me."

"Blake." I swallow back the tears her words bring. "I don't deserve your friendship."

"*You* don't get to decide that." Her fingers dig into my shoulder. "*I* do."

"I'm not worthy."

The laugh that bursts from her is short and sharp, a scrape over my nerve endings that puts every hair on my body on end.

"You don't get to decide that either. My friendship is mine to give, not anyone's to take."

"I betray—"

"No. The only thing you did was close yourself off from me. From everyone. We never would have judged you. Least of all me. Take a close look at those who love you, no one has stopped the way they feel in spite of you shutting yourself away."

"How can anyone love me when I hate myself?"

"I don't think you really hate yourself. I think you hate what happened and the way you dealt with it. Time to come out of hiding and live again, Bran."

I've been here so long, ignored everything outside of this little house in the woods for months and months. Hell, I don't even know how long it is. Two years? Three?

No. Yesterday would have been Laura's third birthday. Not quite three years then. Over two years of hiding away, licking my wounds. Letting the cuts Celeste inflicted fester.

And they have festered.

Fuck.

I need to get back in control.

I need to stop letting her dictate my life.

Hiding out, cutting myself off from everyone I once relied on has done nothing to help me get past the circle of hell my life is—no, *was*. Because it is in the past, my life is no longer being sucked into the depths of hell.

But it's not anything else either.

The coward I am has done nothing to move on, to pick up the pieces and go on.

And I need to do that. Pick up the pieces, fit them together, and get back to living.

Except I don't know where to go from here—how to live when the life I envisioned was destroyed by lies, and the life I was living before it was cruelly ripped away, was someone else's.

I know I have to claw my way back. Have to find the right path, not to where I was but to where I should be now, where I can reclaim myself and possibly the sport I loved. I just...

"I don't know how to live anymore."

"Good thing you've got a friend to help you, a family who loves you. And a multi-million dollar contract ready to sign."

The laugh that leaves me sounds rusty and pulls at muscles in my gut I haven't used in too long to remember. "You had to dangle the contract."

"It's why I'm here."

I look over my shoulder, lock my eyes on hers. "Is that the only reason you're here?"

"Yes. No." Blake sighs, her gaze moving out to the driveway. "It's a see-saw of both. I'm here in my professional capacity as assistant coach and co-owner of the Rogues, and I'm here because I'm your friend. I love you. Neither of those were shut off because you shut an invisible door in my face."

"You can't say you love me. I've done everything to prove I'm not worthy of that."

"You don't get it, Branton. *You* don't get to decide if you're worthy of someone else's love or friendship or affection or whatever. *They* do."

She doesn't let me argue. Spins so fast she slips and bumps the edge of the doorframe with her shoulder as she rushes back inside.

Except she didn't turn fast enough for me to miss the sadness, the disappointment, in her eyes. And that guts me as deeply as the moment I decided to cut her from my life years ago.

Celeste had demanded I break off a number of previous connections. And while I'd done it, I hadn't done it for her.

Although I won't deny it had given me a level of peace to let her believe I'd complied. What I'd really done was protect the people who meant the most to me from the venom my *wife*— the mother of my child—seemed to splash in every direction.

The only thing I'd succeeded in doing was hurting everyone I cared about.

Something I continue to do every day I spend hiding out here.

Because Blake is right.

I am hiding out.

I can't bring myself to face the people I disappointed and hurt in my efforts not to.

I should never have kept them in the dark. Should have reached out the second Celeste had shown me that positive pregnancy test and said the baby was mine.

BLAKE

I don't make breakfast.

Instead I lock myself away in my room and go over countless files of stats and personal information on the players on the potential Rogues shortlist.

Our plan is to move through the shortlist and once we've exhausted that, start on the longer one we compiled in the event we can't get who we believe will be the best fit for the Rogues and have holes in the roster to fill.

It's an attempt to ignore the turmoil of emotions my encounter with Bran caused. A defense mechanism.

I didn't mean to tell him I love him. Shouldn't have told him. But it's hard to keep the truth from coming out when I see him struggling so much. My heart aches with the need to soothe him. To take away his hurt and release him from the prison he's put himself in. In spite of the pain doing so could cause me.

I've heard him moving around on the other side of my closed door but he hasn't knocked and I haven't gone out to see what he's doing.

I'm frightened another interaction like this morning will have me packing my bag and leaving.

The urge is there, riding that see-saw of emotions I've been on since I arrived.

Leave.

Stay.

Leave.

Stay.

It's hard to distinguish my true desire when fear of the known and unknown has me in fight or flight mode.

The instinctive knowledge I once had of Bran is gone. Tainted by the abrupt end to our relationship, by the pain and distrust his actions caused.

I've never struggled with a decision the way I am now. My instincts, the gut feelings that have seen me through nail biting hockey games, through the launch of Rogue sportswear and now the Rogue NHL team, have deserted me.

I'm not getting anywhere with my brain and emotions going round and round in circles.

I'm tempted to call someone. Who is anyone's guess, but I need to bounce my thoughts, my ideas on how to handle Bran —my relationship with him—the offer to play for the Rogues, off someone, and I can't do that with just anyone.

Whomever I call has to be impartial and know our history, be discreet...

I reach for my phone and hit Mom's contact before my brain catches up with my actions.

Of course.

I don't know why I didn't think of her first. She's the only person I can safely have this discussion with. Years ago that would have been someone else, the very person I need to talk about.

The call barely makes it through the first ring before she answers.

"Is this a, I'm five minutes out, keep Dad busy call, or a can you find something to placate Dad with when I tell him I'm not stopping by call?"

Laughing, I say, "Neither. It's a girl who needs her mom's advice call."

"My advice? This is new."

"It is not! I ask you for advice all the time."

"Not about hockey... Oh." Her voice takes on a hushed tone. "Is he bad?"

"No. Contrary to his last days in the public spotlight, he is not drunk off his ass."

"He doesn't have to be fall-down drunk to be bad."

"Okay, I'll accept that. Physically, he's good. From what I can see, he's taken care of himself well in the last few years. Probably better than he had before he came here to hide. Mentally..." I can't keep the sigh in. "I don't know. He said a few things last night that have me questioning everything we know. The reasons we thought he did what he did, why he's here."

"Do we really know anything? Branton removed himself from all our lives and other than the occasional glimpse in the media before the baby was born, mainly the games he played and of course the tragedy that unfolded, we don't really know all that much about that time in his life."

"True. But what he said makes me think everything we *do* know is a lie."

"And what about that bothers you? That he lied? That you don't know the truth? That he stopped confiding in you?"

I mull that over. Roll each question around to see how it makes me feel. "All of it? Maybe that last part more. I don't know, Mom, that's why I called you."

"Okay, then let's talk it out. I know you told me you two never crossed the line of friendship but it was obvious both of you wanted to."

"We had plans."

"What plans?"

"To establish our careers. First."

"I don't understand why either of you thought you had to be single to do that."

"We both had busy training schedules, games, and we lived in different cities."

"That would have been hard to navigate but I watched you both grow up. I know the two of you would have been able to make it work. If you really wanted to."

"I guess we didn't want it bad enough. Maybe it was never meant to happen the way we thought."

"A lot of things in life don't happen the way we think they will, Blake. It doesn't stop us from living, from working hard, from going after what we want. You've done it before, have the failures and successes to show for it. You just need to decide what you want now."

"Bran."

"For the Rogues."

"Yes..."

"I hear that pause. You want that and more. The question you need to ask yourself is are you prepared for the hard work and possible failure, because if you're calling me, I'm assuming you already know it's going to be hard and you might not succeed."

"He hates himself. Thinks we should all hate him. Thinks he doesn't deserve our support or love."

"He needs to see a therapist. Can you convince him to come here? Your father isn't qualified but with his years of captaining and coaching hockey teams I think he'd be able to help Branton get his head straightened out a bit and we can see about getting him in to see someone while you're here. Have them come to the house so no one knows."

"I want to come there. It's what I planned to do when I came up here. And you're right, I think whatever we do, outside of our circle, it needs to be kept quiet, away from prying eyes and possible media exposure."

"When do you think you'll get here? You're in Parry Sound, right?"

"Bran wants to stay here for a week. He said he'll sign the contract to play for the Rogues if I stay with him here for a week first."

"Do you want to do that?"

"I think I should. I don't want to leave here without at least working out where we stand with each other. Outside of the Rogues."

"And I think you have to do that before you can let him sign that contract."

Mom is right, as usual. "I was afraid of that."

Her laughter puts a smile on my face. "You just wanted me to tell you what you already know."

"No. I didn't think about therapy until you mentioned it."

"I notice you're not arguing the rest of it."

"I shouldn't have called. Could have just talked to the wall."

"You can always call and use me as a sounding board, Blake. I like it when you do. It's a change from all you kids going to Dad every time you need an ear or support."

"It isn't like that."

"Oh, I know. He's the hockey expert. It would have been stupid for any of you to come to me for advice on that and I didn't raise stupid kids."

I can hear the grin in her voice and a rush of love fills me. "I love you, Mom."

"I love you too, baby. But let me remind you of the other kind of kids I raised."

A grin stretches my lips. "What other kind did you raise?"

"The brave kind. The fly in the face of fear kind. The kind who aren't afraid to get things wrong. The kind that know a win isn't guaranteed but go after it anyway."

"I have to fix me and Bran before I can sign him to the team."

"Yes. And you knew that without me telling you but I'm so glad you called."

"I have to agree to this week. Spend the time with him and tear off every bandage until all our wounds are aired."

"Yes, if you want to go with that gruesome analogy, that's exactly what you have to do. If you can fix your friendship, whatever form it takes, great; if not, you have to decide if you can work with him as a player on the team you're coaching."

"And if I can't fix us and I can't do the second?"

"Then you have to let him go for good this time."

Mom's words sit heavy in my chest, the weight making it hard to draw in breath.

I thought I'd let Bran go before, sure I was forced to, but the result was the same. He wasn't in my life. It was easy to forget the pain when he wasn't there as a daily reminder of what was no longer an option.

Can I live without him? Yes.

Can I live with him around and not have him? I don't know.

Everything in me has always believed we could fix what he broke if only we had the chance, but with the revelations he's hinted, at I'm no longer so sure.

Whatever happens, Mom is right.

If we can't fix us and I can't work with him afterward, then I'll have no choice.

I'll have to let him go for good this time.

BRANTON

When I finally ventured inside this morning to find no sign of
Blake and her door firmly shut, I was disappointed.

Relieved.

I knew, if I wanted to make things right, tell her the details
of my life since I cut her out of it, I had to give us both some
space. A breather. For now.

Well, mainly me but I'm sure she appreciates not having to
deal with me for a while.

After putting together an omelet and leaving half in the
oven with a note on the counter for Blake, I packed a bag with
water and a couple of protein bars and set out on a four-hour
hike.

Once I broke free of the trees bordering the back of the
property, I stuck to the shoreline, walked for two hours, my
mind running over everything that had happened in the last
day, before I turned around and headed back to the house. The
same thoughts swirling in my head.

I'd like to say the walk did me good—cleared my mind—
but other than getting in some physical exercise, I'm still left

with a head full of confusion and a heartache so sharp if I hadn't already lived with the pain for the last few years, I'd think I was having a heart attack.

As I move through the trees, getting closer to the house, anxiety tightens my chest, squeezes my lungs. There's a thread of excitement too. So many mixed emotions at the thought of seeing Blake again.

Of not seeing her.

The closer I get, the quicker my steps and heart rate, the pulse pounding in my ears masking every other sound. It's not until I'm about fifty feet deep in the trees at the back of the house that I realize I can hear music. A thumping beat that mimics my heart.

I know neither of my neighbors are close enough for the sound to travel this far and I've never heard more than the occasional door or axe hitting wood from either of them anyway.

It has to be Blake.

And relief washes over me so fast I stumble.

She didn't leave.

I had hoped my return might go unnoticed, the fleeting thought of slipping inside and going directly to my room without bumping into her had crossed my mind, not that I want to avoid her. Although she sure as shit probably wants to avoid me.

And while I want to give her space, I'm more than thankful she's still here. I didn't know what to expect when I got back to the house, but I need to be honest with myself—and her— finding her gone wouldn't have surprised me.

I'd hate it but I know, once again, it would be me that pushed her away.

Then again, I should know better.

It's Blake.

She isn't one to back away from a challenge or when she thinks I'm being an idiot and need some sense talked into me. The numerous unanswered phone calls over the last few years are proof of that.

In spite of the depressing thoughts I've lived with all day, that last one brings a smile to my face.

How different would my life be, would things have gone, if I'd answered just one of her calls? If I'd let her tell me all the ways I was fucking up?

I'm not sure what it says about me that I got off—hell, still get off—on Blake Watts giving me a lecture on the ways I'm being dumb. Anyone else giving me a stern talking to—calling me on my bullshit—always gets my back up, but Blake?

Hell, no.

Blake delivering a dressing-down makes me want to strip us both naked and find a bed to roll around on together.

With the imagined naked Blake in my head, I break through the last of the trees into the backyard to discover what the music is all about. And stop short at the sight before me.

Blake, dressed in nothing but her underwear, which if I could move closer, I'm sure I'd see is not underwear but a set of activewear that no doubt bears the Rogue sportswear label, dancing across the deck.

She has the heaters blazing and the sun has been out most of the day so while it might not be considered warm, it's not that cold either. Add the heat radiating down from the deck roof and she's probably toasty with the way she's busting out her moves.

Instead of getting closer like every instinct is screaming for me to do, I stand perfectly still and watch her. And me and my dick are reminded of how sexy she is—how much I've always wanted her.

It's interesting to note I haven't had any kind of input from my sex drive in years, can't remember the last time I rubbed one out—before Celeste?—and now it's yelling loud and clear how it feels.

"You know in some places you have to pay to watch," Blake shouts above the music.

I'm startled and a bark of laughter catches in my throat when her words register.

I had no idea she knew I was here. Her back is to me and has been the whole time, and there's no chance she heard me over the music.

She dances over to the table where a few taps on her phone has the music stopping abruptly. "I saw you in the window," she says at a normal volume as she turns to face me, resting her butt against the table, arms crossed over her chest, the bare expanse of her belly holding my gaze captive for a moment.

When I can pull it away, I glance at the wall of windows and see a perfectly clear reflection of the backyard, myself included. "Oh."

"Good hike?"

Returning my gaze to her, I find her studying me. "Yeah. Good exercise, fresh air."

"You hike often?"

"Have since I got here."

Her gaze moves away from me, traveling along the tree line. "You mind if I tag along next time?"

Something pinches in my chest. I know what it is. Ache and longing and regret. We used to hike all over her parents' property together. Swallowing hard, I have to force the word out. "Sure."

"I made lunch. Soup." She pushes off the table and waves toward the house. "It should be ready in about fifteen minutes if you want to grab a quick shower."

When I say my walk was good exercise, I'm not talking

exercise exercise. In the hours I've been gone, I've barely worked up a sweat. "I'm good. Took an easy path today."

"Mind if I jump in real quick? These heaters on high are like a sauna."

I grin. "Is that why you stripped off?"

"Ha!" Shaking her head she scoops up her phone and a hoodie from the back of a chair. "No. I did a sixty-minute hot yoga session before the rave party started."

My eyes are now on her thick thighs, my mind wondering how soft the skin is there. It looks silky smooth. Shaking my head, I try to clear my thoughts and focus on something that isn't a practically naked Blake. "Need me to do anything to get lunch on the table?"

"Set it?"

"Are you asking me to set it or if I should set it?"

With a shrug she says, "Both, I guess. I was planning to spoon out a bowl and come back out here but now that I have company I should probably put in more effort."

"You've done enough by making the soup. You didn't have to."

"I didn't make it for you, Bran. I need to eat too."

Ouch. The barb is a direct hit I didn't see coming. Although I'm sure she didn't mean it that way.

I have no right to take offense at her words, to be hurt by them. Except I am. Because I want to have her care again. I want her to think of me when she does things. I want it with a bone-deep ache that I have no right to feel.

I shut her out of my life. I can't expect her to come back like nothing happened. Like I didn't hurt her in the worst way.

I have so much to make up for. So many tattered threads of our friendship I need to mend. A process I know will take time. And if it takes me the rest of my life to do it, I'll gladly spend my days fixing what I broke because she's worth it.

Neither of us are the people we were before. What we've been through has changed us—me more than her—and the first step to re-establishing our relationship is getting to know each other again.

"Are you still strict with your diet? Now that you're not playing."

"Who said I'm not playing?"

"You quit the team, coached the Canadian national team. I just assumed..."

"I play pickup games whenever I can. And I do a lot of one-on-one training with a number of professional players since I quit. I'm probably in better shape now than I was before. It's amazing what a few extra hours of sleep can do."

"And now you're training the Rogues full-time."

"Not yet. But I will be. Walker and I need to put together our plan. We haven't had much time to talk about it yet. But I know his style, I think we'll fit well."

I know Blake, grew up beside her on the ice, watched her streak across it for years. And the years I played on the same team as Walker have given me insight on how his mind works. "You two are going to crush it."

"That's the plan." Taking a step toward the house she says, "I'll grab that shower so we can eat."

"I'll set the table."

She eyes me and I can see her mind rolling something around. Pulling in a slow breath I wait, but in the end she gives me a smile laced with sadness before she turns and heads inside.

I don't know if it's relief or disappointment that fills my chest. The last few minutes may have felt like old times but I'm not a fool. I know this isn't what it once was. Our lifelong friendship broke apart when I pushed her and everyone else in my life away.

The minute Celeste came to me and told me she was pregnant, I made the worst decision of my life. I knew it then, but I did it anyway.

And instead of going to the people who had my back, the people I trusted, I went it alone, took a path that led me through the fires of hell before spitting me out here.

BLAKE

I don't know what to expect when I leave the bathroom after my shower, but it isn't the scent of baking bread.

Dumping my dirty clothes in my room I follow my nose to the kitchen to find Bran pulling a loaf of crusty looking bread out of the oven. "How the hell did you make that so quickly?"

"Shit!" He bobbles the pan as he puts it on the stovetop. "You scared the crap out of me, woman!"

"Sorry." I move closer, take a big breath of yeasty air. "But how did you make that so quick?"

"I have a routine. I've always got dough ready to bake."

I can't keep the shock from my face or my voice. "You bake bread?"

"Didn't I tell you I made the loaf we had yesterday?" he asks as he flips the bread out of the pan onto a cooling rack. "I could swear I did."

"Eh..." I try to remember but the scent of fresh bread and the bubbling soup have my stomach growling. "You might have. I can't remember."

"Yeah, well, I bake a couple of times a week. Once a loaf gets low I get the next batch ready to throw in the oven."

"Very domestic of you." I grin. The idea that Bran, the boy who used to bitch about washing dishes or picking up his dirty clothes—my gaze darts around the house.

Nothing is out of place.

There are no dirty dishes in the sink or clothes on the floor or empty pizza boxes overflowing the bin. "You're very domesticated now..."

His movements stop abruptly, his whole body going rigid, and I swear, he isn't breathing.

I want to take back the words, suck them back down my throat, and I don't know why. It's just the tension in the air, it feels heavy, broken with razor sharp edges, and I'm—

"When no one else in the house behaves like an adult, there's no choice."

His words sound like boots grinding on gravel and the rawness of them has me hunching my shoulders, pulling back without taking a step. "I—"

"How many slices do you want?"

The abrupt change in topic makes my head spin for a second but then I get it. He's revealed another piece of the puzzle that is—*was*—his life without me in it. A hard piece. One he wouldn't have given me if I'd kept my mouth shut.

"Don't."

My head snaps up, my eyes colliding with Bran's. "What?"

"Don't beat yourself up. It's not your fault. And I don't want you walking on eggshells. I'll handle anything you throw at me." He shakes his head. "God knows I've already handled the worst."

"I wish—"

"You and me both, Blake, but we can't change anything that happened before. Only what might happen now." Indicating the cupboard behind me with a lift of his chin, he says, "Get the bowls. Dish up the soup—that smells fantastic by the way, and let's go eat out in the sauna."

He says the last with a cheeky smirk that reminds me of our childhood. One that has me helpless to stop the curl of my own lips. "I'll turn a couple of them off."

"You don't have to. I don't mind the heat and I should probably get used to it, right?"

"You thinking of leaving your hidey-hole?"

"You don't think it's time?"

"I'm the wrong person to ask."

"Oh?"

"I don't think you should have ever hidden yourself or what was happening." I have to swallow the emotions threatening to burst out of me. "I would never have judged you."

"You know, the more I see you, the more I realize it wasn't about anyone else, especially you, judging me. I'd already judged myself."

"Someone wise once told me we are our own worst critics."

"Your dad." Bran's smile stretches wide. "I've missed his sage words of wisdom."

"Good. Because that's where we're going when we leave here."

He eyes me closely. "In a week."

"Yes. One week. I'll give you the week you asked for."

"And I'll sign your contract." His gaze drills into mine, the force of it taking my breath. "With or without the week, I'll sign."

"But—"

"Let's not worry about that now. This bread is toasty warm and your soup smells delicious and I can hear your stomach rumbling from here."

"I am hungry. It's been hours since I came out to find

someone had made me breakfast, left it warming in the oven. Thank you for that, I didn't expect it."

"You're welcome. And thank you for taking care of lunch."

"Maybe we can join forces and take care of dinner together?"

"Absolutely." His gaze turns sad, wistful. "I've missed this."

"This?"

"Being with a friend, sharing meals with someone I care about. For a while, every interaction was a battle in a war I had no hope of winning."

"I'm sorry."

"Don't be. I got myself into the situation. I deserved—"

"Not that. No one deserves what you went through." Neither of us speaks the words and I still don't know the full story but nobody, not even the haters I've dealt with over the years, deserves what Branton has endured.

"Agree to disagree. Now let's get lunch on the table."

"I'll get drinks."

"Water for me. I might not have worked up a sweat on my hike, but I still need to hydrate."

"Well, I did work up a sweat, so two waters coming right up, then I'll dish out the soup, or should we just take the pot out and serve ourselves at the table?"

"We can do that. There's a square tile on the table that we can put the hot pot on."

"Okay. I'll take the soup out and come back for the rest." As I do what I said, I try not to dwell on the things Bran revealed.

If he and Celeste were always fighting, why the hell were they together?

Nothing is making sense and I have so many questions. Questions I'm not sure I want the answers to. Except this is

Bran. The boy I grew up with. The boy who was my friend. The boy who turned into the man I fell in love with. The man I thought I'd spend my life with.

The man I let push me away when everything in me was screaming to get closer.

I didn't push back. I should have pushed back. I should never have accepted the silence between us. Not even sure why I did. It wasn't what I wanted.

And yet I didn't even push when his world fell apart. I just sat back and wished I could be there for him. What kind of friend does that make me?

Bran blames himself, but aren't I just as much to blame?

My inactions speak for themselves.

I'll need to think hard, look deep, to work out why I let things go the way I did.

After talking with Mom, and the conversations I've had with Bran so far, I'm not sure I can let him go. And the warning he gave, about not thinking he's pretty after I know everything doesn't do a thing to make me want to either.

I'm not even sure I let him go before. I stayed away, focused on my life, but did I really let him go?

The feelings rising to the surface now suggest I didn't.

It only makes me want to get closer, get back to where we were before Celeste came into the picture.

"I cut four pieces each. I'll eat that many and I know you could pack away the carbs when you played..."

"Four's good," I say as I pass him on my way back into the house. "I'll just grab our drinks."

"There's ice if you want it. I put a tray in the freezer this morning."

I can't help laughing.

"What's funny?" Bran calls out.

"Just picturing how yesterday would have been different if you'd had ice in your freezer."

"Oakley would have loaded the bucket with ice instead of water?" he asks from right behind me.

I didn't realize he'd followed me back inside and the sound of his voice so close sends a shiver down my spine. "Ah, no. She would have added the ice to the water and waited a few minutes for the ice to chill the water before dumping it over your head."

"Cruel, cruel woman."

"She's not."

He holds up a hand. "No. She's not. I know that. I was joking. Obviously I'm so rusty at this interacting with others thing, it didn't come out right."

"I don't think you're that rusty and it was probably fine but I'm a little sensitive when it comes to the women of KAW. We've dealt with a lot of shit-talk over the years and I'm sure we'll be dealing with a hell of a lot more now that the world knows about the Rogues."

"The world? Or is it a select few who will dig at you?"

"The latter. I think most hockey fans will embrace the new team, and honestly, I don't need to defend our choices or plans. What we've done so far, what we're planning for the future, is about more than the Rogues. I think once we're established, the team on the ice, people will see that."

"If they don't, fuck 'em."

I grin. "Keep that attitude, because when the world finds out you're signing on with the Rogues, you're bound to get some of that shit flung your way."

"Then I should tell you everything so there aren't any skeletons lurking in dark closets."

"I'm not afraid of dark closets."

"What about the skeletons?"

"Those don't scare me either."

"Good. Because I've got a graveyard full of them. Real and otherwise."

Branton

We've both finished a bowl and served ourselves a second of Blake's chicken and vegetable soup when I start to talk. I didn't lie. She needs to know all the skeletons in my graveyard.

Some will be easier than others to reveal and the coward that I am, I start with the easiest.

"I don't remember it."

Blake looks at me, her spoon halfway to her mouth. "What?"

"Fucking Celeste. Making Laura."

She lowers the spoon back to her bowl. "Oh."

"Yeah. Never been blackout drunk before." The memories of waking in bed with Celeste plastered to my back and no recollection of how I got there, flashes through my head. "Or since."

I can't stand to stay in my seat, to look at her when I tell her the rest, so I shove my chair back and walk over to the deck railing. Wrapping my fingers around the wood, I stare off into the trees without really seeing them.

The emotions of that long ago morning assault me, and the

sympathy in Blake's eyes only add to the guilt I already feel. I don't deserve her compassion. I don't deserve anyone's.

"Not even in the alcohol fueled days after I told the doctors they could kill Laura," I mutter.

"Bran."

Blake wraps her arms around me from behind. How she got so close without my knowledge, I don't know, but the gentle strength of her hold eases some of the ache in my chest.

"You didn't kill Laura. None of you killed Laura. She was already gone. The accident took her away long before you had to make that decision."

"My brain knows that but..." I swallow the bile rising in my throat. "I gave them permission to turn the machines off."

Blake's hold tightens. "Without those machines, she wasn't alive."

"I *know* that. Except holding her..." I scrunch my eyes closed, try to wipe away the memories of Laura, her small body warm against my bare chest where I cradled her in my arms in those final moments. "She was so tiny. I was supposed to protect her."

"You weren't Laura's only protector. She had her mother."

And that's the sticking point. Celeste never wanted her. Never wanted to be a mom. "She didn't come to me to be a father to her child."

"But—"

"She wanted me to pay for an abortion." Those words, just the thought of what Celeste had planned, make me want to vomit.

"Oh."

"I paid her to have the baby, to marry me. *Stay* married to me and have the baby."

"Paid..."

"Yes. I paid for her to have the child." I squeeze my eyes

closed again. Can see the look of horror on Celeste's face at my suggestion. "I paid her to marry me and have the baby. Then I paid her to put my name on the birth certificate. Once I'd paid for one thing, she had me over a barrel. It was going to cost me thirty million to get her to sign over parental rights. Another fifty to sign the divorce papers."

"You were getting divorced?"

"Trying." If only Celeste had waited longer than six weeks to step out. "She blew that up by hooking up with another player. Or attempting to, anyway."

"I don't understand why she would—"

"She didn't love me. I certainly didn't love her. But the baby? The baby I loved with everything in me. I wanted her."

"Of course you did. She was your child."

"She was mine. In every way that counts." I don't want to go down that path. Not today. I want to explain why I married a woman I didn't love when I hadn't married the one I did. "She wouldn't just take money to have the baby. She wanted marriage or she'd find a way to get the money to get rid of it, her words. It cost me. Everything cost me but that was what she wanted. A source of money she thought was unending."

"That's awful. But, Bran, you had no choice but to do what you did. For Laura."

"Maybe, maybe not. Anyway, we went to the closest court house and got all the paperwork sorted, went back the next day and made it official. We moved into a house I bought and turned it into a battlefield. Celeste fought me on everything. From the color on the walls to the car she wanted me to buy her. Everything." A bark of laughter burst from my chest. "Even the brand of fucking toilet paper was an argument."

"I'm sorry."

"Me too. It could have been different. If she'd embraced

being a mother but ultimately it wasn't what she wanted and she blamed me for that too."

"It takes two to make a baby. She had no right to blame you for getting pregnant."

"No. She didn't." The urge to tell Blake why Celeste had no reason wells up, but I can't go there yet. If I'm going to purge my guilt, free myself from the regret, I need to walk her through it from the beginning.

Fuck. Who am I kidding? I need to do it in stages or I'll be reaching for the nearest bottle and not stopping until it's empty and my hand is on the next.

"Her plan was to have the baby and leave after her six-week checkup. Except she never made that appointment. Instead, she snuck out of the house and met up with Carl Burgan, defense player for the Knights. I guess he thought it would be a quick hookup. They'd done it before, except Celeste's body had changed. Carrying a baby is hard on a woman's body. Carl wasn't happy with the changes. Must have said some horrible things because she came home ranting and raving about us ruining her body, her life."

"You married her, gave her a home, a daughter."

"She'd take the house, not me, not the daughter."

"What?"

"She wanted the house in the divorce, she didn't want anything to do with Laura."

I can feel Blake shake her head against my back where her forehead rested. "What mother doesn't want—"

"One who never wanted." I have to take a deep breath to continue. "I paid her to have the baby, remember?"

"How much?"

"Ten million."

"Bran."

"I know. I dropped five on her to get her to the court

house, ten to have the baby and I had to be on top of her because I'd given her money, money she could have used to abort the baby."

"She wouldn't."

"She threatened to often enough I couldn't be sure. There was always something she wanted or wanted to do, or me to do, it was easy to get my compliance with the threat of the baby."

"You did it all for the baby."

"I did. And I'd probably do it again."

"What happened to stop her from signing the divorce papers? You said you were trying to get divorced."

"Carl happened. Whatever he said made her think she would be better off staying with me. Not that we were together in any way other than on paper. I never touched her after we were married. I didn't even kiss her at the ceremony. Barely held her hands during the quick service."

"You didn't..."

"No. I didn't. I couldn't. She wasn't meant to be the woman with my ring on her finger. Wasn't meant to be living in my house. I can't to this day, stand referring to her as my wife. If I could wipe it all out, go back in time and erase it all, I would. In a heartbeat."

"Bran."

I turn, put my hands on Blake's shoulders and push her back, finally look her in the eye. "I have never loved, will never love, anyone but you. I hate what I did, what I allowed to happen, hate it all with a bone deep burn that threatens to take me under every day. And it was all for nothing."

"It wasn't for nothing. It was for Laura, your daughter. You're not the type of man who could ever turn his back on his own flesh and blood."

"No, I'm not." I lock my gaze on Blake's. I want her to see what I'm feeling when I tell her the rest. "I knew she wasn't mine to keep. When Celeste opted for a c-section and attempted to keep me out of the birth, I knew it would always be like that. And when the nurse handed me the baby and I looked at her, I knew. She wasn't going to be mine to keep but I vowed, with that first touch, that I would do everything I could to protect her for the rest of her life."

This is the hardest thing I've ever had to say out loud. I never told anyone. The doctors know a little of how Laura really got hurt but when Celeste took the easy way out and took her own life within hours of them telling us Laura had no neural function, no brain activity, I kept it inside. Hid the truth from the world because there was no one to punish.

No one but myself.

"The one person I didn't know I had to protect Laura from was her own mother. You were right before. I wasn't responsible for killing Laura. But it wasn't an accident. Celeste killed her. Killed herself. And it wasn't postpartum depression either. It was malicious and with the intent to hurt her, to hurt *me*."

BLAKE

I don't know what to say. I can't fathom how any human can hurt another, never mind a defenseless baby. At the time the media reported about the accident...

"But she fell down the stairs...they tumbled down the stairs. It was an accident. You couldn't have saved them." I know that as well as I know my own name. If Bran could have stopped them, he would have.

"No. We were arguing. Then Laura woke up and Celeste went to get her. I let her. Wanted the break from the yelling and I thought...maybe she was finally feeling maternal. But I heard her. Through the baby monitor. Knew she was going to do something, could hear it in her voice. But I was at the other end of the house and by the time I got there, Laura was crumpled on the floor next to her crib..." he swallows hard, tears rolling down his face. "After, when I went over the video—"

"Oh, Bran."

"I scooped Laura up, knew it was bad, she was like a rag doll in my arms, and I knew I had to get her to the hospital. Fast. Celeste followed me, yelling and screaming and when I didn't listen, she threw herself down the stairs. Begged me to take her with me, to say it was an accident and at that point I just wanted to get Laura to the hospital. She came in the car with me, kept muttering about it being an accident. We went through the motions in emergency, Celeste hysterically telling a bullshit story about falling down the stairs with the baby in her arms, and of course Celeste had the bruises and broken wrist to prove it."

"She lied about how Laura was hurt?"

"I think she knew she was done. Whatever happened, she knew she'd gone too far. And while I was in with Laura and the doctors, she was discharged, her injuries not life threatening or warranting admission. She went home and erased all the security footage from that point until the week before."

"But you—"

"Yes. She didn't know I had a backup. Everything gets stored in cloud storage as it's filmed. All she got was the in-house copies."

"She was never charged with—"

"No. When the police were called because some of the tests were showing it wasn't a simple fall, Celeste and I had already spoken. I knew she'd hurt Laura on purpose, called her on it. When she taunted me with lack of proof I told her about the cloud copies. She lost it. Was completely inconsolable and of course everyone thought she was distraught about Laura. The doctor sedated her and gave her a script for sleeping pills."

"I thought Laura died from a brain injury from a fall. It's what the press reported."

"She didn't. After Celeste's meltdown the police decided to wait before questioning either of us further because the doctors were already talking about Laura's lack of brain activity. When Celeste woke, I made it clear I would use the tapes, would tell the police she deliberately hurt Laura, and she left. I had no idea she'd taken the bottle of sleeping pills with her or that she'd gone straight to the house and swallowed them with two bottles of alcohol. I found her after—" a sob cuts his words off.

"She committed suicide." The devastation Bran must have felt.

"She took the easy way out."

"I don't think it would have been easy."

Bran's laugh is laced with disgust. "Oh, she thought it would be easy. Said as much in the letter she left me. The one explaining everything from our first night together to our last when she wanted to take away the one thing I loved. Laura."

"She must have been depressed or—"

"Celeste was completely cognizant every step of the way. She knew what she was doing, what her actions could cause. She made my life hell to get what she wanted and for the most part she succeeded. Until the last night when she came home after her failed hookup with Carl."

"How did you know they'd hooked up before?"

"He told me. At training. Before Laura was born. And after everything had happened, he told me about meeting up with Celeste. Made it out like she came on to him that last time but he couldn't give an explanation as to why he was at the hotel they met at."

"The Knights traded him around the time..." I can't bring myself to say Laura died.

"No. He asked for the trade. Gerald Cantrell agreed it would be a good idea. It was one of the last things he did for me before he died. The other was releasing me from my contract without penalty and refusing to bring charges against me for assault when I decked a couple of the training staff and coaches at my last game."

"And then you came here."

"No. Not right away. I locked myself in the house for a

couple of months first. Ignored everyone. Gannon Byrd turned up on my doorstep one day, got in somehow. He handed me a key and an address and told me if I wanted to get lost, I should do it for real." His gaze moves over the yard. "He knew what he was talking about. This is the perfect place to get lost."

"Except you're not lost, you know exactly where you are. You're hiding and you have every right to do so. Bran." I slip a hand over his, where it rests on my shoulder. "You need to come out of hiding now. You need to reclaim your life. No one expects you to forget Laura but you also shouldn't forget yourself. You deserve to find peace, find happiness again."

"I don't know if that's possible."

"Of course it is. And no one can or would expect you to be happy all the time."

"I need help. I don't think I can do it on my own. No, I *know* I can't do it on my own." He waves his other hand around us. "Look where doing it myself has gotten me."

"I think you did fine. There's no timeline for grief and you have more than that to work through." I'm not sure if I should bring it up now, but Mom's words play in my head and even if I can't get him to agree to it right this minute, I can float the idea, get him used to it. "I think you should see someone trained in grief counseling."

"I don't—"

"Not now, when you're ready. One thing at a time. You've told me what happened, why you married Celeste after you told me we should wait and as much as I hate that, hate that you made us wait then went and tied yourself to someone else, I understand it. I would have supported it."

"No, Blake, no. You can't think the way I dealt with Celeste and the baby was right."

"I can. You're a very instinctual person, Bran, if you felt

marrying her was the only option then it was. She would have gone through with her threat, I have no doubt about that."

"Manipulation and threats were her standard. In many ways she used them to isolate me and keep me prisoner to her whims. She's the reason I stopped answering your calls, ignored your family, my friends."

"You're not her captive anymore. But you can't just shake it off. It's unreal of you or anyone else to expect you to return to normal now that she's out of your life."

"I didn't claim her."

"What? You married her."

"No, not that. Her body. I donated Celeste's body to research. There was no memorial, no burial, no grave."

"She didn't deserve one. You gave those things to Laura. You might not remember most of it but I do, my family—your family—and friends do. We were all there. Watching you break that day and knowing you wouldn't let any of us help was the worst day of my life."

"I'm sorry."

"No." I place my hand over his mouth. "No more sorries. No need to apologize anymore. I won't accept them after this."

"I need to apologize, to tell you how much I regret—"

"Show me."

"Show you?"

"Yes. Show me! Stop hiding here. Stop keeping everything inside. Stop thinking you have to carry this burden alone. What happened to Laura was not your fault. You are not to blame for Laura getting hurt, for having to make the tough decision and tell the doctors to turn the machines off. That is not on your shoulders."

"But—"

"No. *Not* your fault."

"I don't think I can do it."

"You can. You will."

"But what if I can't?"

"I'll be here to help. I can't do it for you, but I can hold your hand or listen when you need to talk or whatever it is you need to come back from this place you've put yourself. This isn't how your life should be. It's not what you deserve. I'll fight for you, Bran, but you have to fight for you too."

"I can't ask you to—"

"You're not asking! I'm offering, but you have to want my help. You have to want what I'm helping you go after. I can put everything I have into it and get nowhere if you're not fighting for it too."

"I don't know what I want."

I can tell he does. He's too fearful to reach for it yet. "You do, deep down you do."

"What if what I want is impossible?"

"You won't know until you try. When we were young, there were days when Dad worked us until our legs were jelly and we thought we'd never be good enough, never be tough enough, to make it to a professional level, but we did. We did it because we wanted it and we worked hard for it. Getting your life back isn't going to be easy and I have no doubt there will be days where you'll think you don't have it in you, but I can guarantee you do, I know you, and when you need a little bit more steam to keep going, I'll be there to share mine."

"I can't ask that of you. Not after everything. Except I'm going to. Because, Blake, as much as I don't think I deserve your support, I don't think I can come back from this without you."

"Good thing you won't have to."

"And if I want to get us back on the path we were on before I let Celeste detour us?"

"One day at a time. Let's get you out of your hidey-hole and back to life, then we'll revisit that question."

"That's not a no."

"It's not. But it's not a yes either, Bran. So much has happened and I'm not ready to make a decision about what type of friendship we'll have going forward. For now, I'm an old friend with a new offer."

"And I get this week here with you before we venture out into the world."

"Well, not the world exactly. At the end of this week, we're doing something you need to do first. We're going home."

Branton

We're going home.

I have no idea what that means anymore. I thought I was building one with my daughter only for that to be ripped away.

Not once but twice.

I haven't lied to Blake, but an omission is a lie, isn't it?

There were a couple of times I could have revealed everything except what I have to tell her could destroy her—her family—more than me pushing them from my life did.

It's the last skeleton in my graveyard and I'm the only one breathing who knows.

Last man standing.

Sometimes I feel like I'm the only one in the world. The only one to feel the pain I live with every day.

Do I have the courage to speak the truth?

Should I when the truth will have more people living with the pain of losing Laura?

"You've gone quiet again."

Turning, I find Blake watching me. "Just thinking about your family."

"They're yours too."

"Not really. I lost the right to claim them when I cut them out of my life, didn't I?"

"That's for each of them to decide. But I know for a fact Dad and Mom would never turn their backs on you."

"I feel bad for not reaching out. For not answering their calls."

"Are you going to tell them the truth?"

"When I apologize, yes. I think I have to."

"Will you do that when we go this week?"

"I should." My gaze moves off to the trees and the sunbeams playing through the leaves. "I'm not sure I have the guts to do it though."

"I'll be there if you want."

"I don't want to lean on you. I shouldn't need to lean on you."

"And you won't have to forever. But right now, if you need me there, I will be."

"You shouldn't forgive me so easily."

"Everyone who knows, or believes they know, how close we were thinks I should never forgive you. I don't have the same view. As I see it, you did the only thing you could to protect your child. I can't fault you for that. There's no forgiveness necessary for that. I do have to forgive you for not at least explaining why you had to step away from us. If you'd told me, I would have understood."

"You're amazing." I've never hidden my awe of Blake, how much I admire her. Even when my infatuation led to embarrassing teenage moments, she never once made me feel bad about my obvious feelings.

Her handling of her younger brothers' best friend's inept attempts to get her attention only made me love her deeper.

And now, with everything I've put us through, she's still

dealing with me and my issues with grace, with care, with her ability to forgive.

"I think you're pretty amazing too. It's why I know you didn't do anything to hurt anyone. Not on purpose."

"I still should have shown more care."

"Sounds to me like you were barely surviving. Not sure you had the resources to show more care."

"If I knew then what I know now, I would have done things differently."

"Wouldn't we all? Hindsight is wonderful for making better choices but I believe you made the best choice you could at the time with the information you had. Would I have liked a heads up? Sure. Did I deserve one? Maybe. But we hadn't made definite plans, we'd skirted the subjects, talked abstractly about the future and what we wanted without really committing to them."

"I felt committed."

"I did too. And yet, neither of us fought for those commitments. We let them go."

"I shoved them to the back of my mind. Tried to not think about them or you. I couldn't. It hurt too much to do it and I was already battling heartache every day."

"You're still battling it. I know me telling you to stop won't make it happen but stop beating yourself up about the way things ended between us. I'm letting it go. You need to do the same."

"I repeat, you're amazing. I don't deserve your loyalty or friendship, but I'll spend the rest of my life earning it if you'll let me."

"You don't have to earn it, I'm freely giving it."

"Why?"

"You know why."

I do. It's why I want her here, why I want to share all my

skeletons even if they hurt her. Because this time I'll be there to support her, to guide her through the pain I unwillingly inflict with the secret I need to tell her.

"What are we cooking for dinner?"

Her change of subject gives me a reprieve. A few more hours, days if I'm lucky, where I can hold the final piece of the past I need to share with her. "Want to go out?"

"Leave here?" She points to the ground at her feet.

"Yes."

"You mean go somewhere else? Leave the property?"

I grin. "Yes, smart ass, leave the property."

"Okay. What does this little town have to offer?"

"Not so little."

"Not big either."

"No, but there are plenty of choices. Pizza, seafood, Italian, burgers, there's a number of bar and grills if you want a steak."

"How are we getting there? I didn't see a car in the driveway."

"It's in the garage."

"Hiding like its owner?"

"No. It's not mine. Gannon keeps it here for tooling around in."

"All right, we have transport, now what do we want to have? Or should we *tool around* and see what takes our fancy?"

"Have you been to Parry Sound before?"

"No. And Walker barely slowed down on the drive through town so I didn't get a good look around. If you're up to showing me, I'd love to see where you've been spending your time."

"You've seen where I've spent my time. The grocery store delivers. I have hardly left the property, except to hike since I got here two years ago."

"You... I... What the hell, Bran!"

"You said I was hiding, and I guess I was." The thought doesn't sit well. I know I put myself here, kept away from my old life, old friends, but until right now I hadn't realized exactly how true Blake's words were. "I need to get my life back," I mutter as I reach for Blake's hand and tug her behind me as I head through the house.

"Where are you taking me?"

"To find my life. To find me."

"Are you lost?"

"I think so. And for a while I was okay with that. Now, not so much."

"And I'm going to be your partner in crime for this life hunt?"

Her question brings me up short. Turning, I study her expression. "You don't want to help me find my new life?"

"What I want isn't what matters, Bran. What do you want?"

"I want to do what you said. Live again. And I want to do it with you."

"As your friend and possibly your coach."

"Definitely my coach. And my friend. But I hope over time I can convince you to let me be more."

"Bran."

"I'm not asking or expecting that now. But I think I should make my intentions clear. I want on your team. I want in your life. And eventually, I want in your bed."

"That's a lot of want."

"I haven't let myself think about anything other than the hell my life was until you showed up with a bucket-wielding Oakley. Now, it's all I can think about. I let someone else dictate who I was, who I should be, then rip it all away, and I didn't have, *couldn't find*, the courage to pull myself out of the dark pit I fell into."

"And you've found that courage?"

"No. I've found the light." I step closer, lift my free hand, and cradle her jaw. "You, Blake. You are my light. You always were. And for a long time, I refused to let you shine on me. I won't be doing that ever again."

Dropping my hand, I give hers a tug with my other and lead her outside, toward the detached garage.

"Shouldn't we get changed? Grab our coats?" she asks, with a small chuckle. "Maybe I could put some shoes on over my socks?"

"What?" I glance back to see her socked feet. "Shit! Sorry. Yes. Let's get coats and boots and whatever else we might need for a night on the town."

"A night on the town? Sounds like I should bring my dancing shoes."

"Do you want to go dancing? I don't know if there's—" Her laughter cuts me off. "Okay, that was a joke. Right?"

Blake nods, her laughter gone but her mouth is still stretched wide. "Yes, that was a joke."

"Told you I was rusty."

"Maybe a little." She pulls on our joined hands. "C'mon, let's get ready and lock up the house. We can spend the afternoon tooling around town in Gannon's car then find somewhere to eat."

The idea of exploring with Blake lights me up like nothing has in too long to remember. "Thank you."

"For?"

"For being you. For helping me. For not hating me."

"I could never hate you."

I hear her, believe she means it, but I'm not sure she'll feel the same when she finds out I unwittingly stole something from her and her family.

BLAKE

Parry Sound is like a lot of towns—big or small—in Canada.

Hockey mad.

Especially so seeing how one of the greatest players of all time was born here.

We didn't even get out of the boat of a car Gannon Byrd owns before the first person approached for an autograph. I'm pretty sure they thought Bran was Gannon at first. Especially after one of the locals mentioned the car once belonged to his late grandmother.

The true hockey fans get a bit flustered and inquisitive when they work out who we are, that we both play—played— professionally. They want to know if we'll play again.

And when the fanatics realize I'm one of the owners of the new expansion team, the questions about Bran and me together get more specific. Is Bran going to play for my team? Who else are we looking to sign? Have we chosen our team colors? Our mascot?

Bran deflects well, in spite of not having been in the spotlight for years. Like riding a bike, the media training he was put through in the past, not to mention the times Dad gave us advice on navigating our celebrity, click into place and I couldn't be more proud of him.

I can see his discomfort, but I'm sure it isn't obvious to anyone else. And for the most part, once we dodge a question or two, people give up digging and offer advice on where to eat, what to see in town.

That's how we find ourselves eating at Mama Jo's. Stepping through the door is like stepping through time. Booths that seat up to six line one wall, square tables surrounded by four chairs fill the center of the room, round stools with shiny legs run the length of the counter on the opposite wall to the booths... the furnishings aren't the only thing pointing to the time-warp crossing the threshold sucks you into.

It's the uniforms the waitresses wear, their hairdos, the soda machine and pie display on the far end of the counter.

If some Hollywood director is looking for authentic sixties diner style they need to go no further, just have to step through the door of Mama Jo's.

Oh, and they need to be sure to order the daily special.

I have it on good authority that everything Mama Jo cooks is worth the price but she puts a unique twist on the daily special that makes it impossible to pass up.

How do I know this? Harold told me. He said it in a whisper, his hand covering his mouth as though someone might read his lips, when he imparted the 'town secret'.

Apparently, they don't give this information to just any old tourist, but seeing how I brought home more than one gold medal for the country, even though I insist on playing my team out of the *south*, I earned the insider knowledge.

I had to hold in my laughter. The smirk on Bran's face didn't help, but I managed to keep a straight face and thank Harold. Promise I would indeed order the daily special.

A special that turns out to be a classic cheeseburger with special sauce and fries, followed by butter tarts with homemade vanilla ice cream. Marg, our waitress, flushes pink when she looks at Bran and the shy smile she sends his way once she's written down our order doesn't go unnoticed either.

When she leaves our booth to put in our order, I lean forward and whisper, "I think you have an admirer."

"Marg? Yeah, she's one of the people I've seen more than once since I've been here. She delivers for the grocery store on Mondays."

"Only Mondays?"

"Yes."

"And how do you know that?"

"Whenever I call in an order, I get a tut-tut if it's not Monday. Arthur, the grocery store owner, seems to think Marg and I would make a good pair and isn't afraid to let me know."

"And how does he come to that conclusion?"

"I'm told Marg and Arthur's daughter are best friends and Marg has mentioned on more than one occasion how nice she thinks I am."

"You tip well."

"What?"

"I bet you tip the delivery person well, that would make anyone smitten."

Chuckling, Bran mutters, "I'm sure it's a little more than that."

"She's got to be twice your age."

"I like older women." He winks, the smirk on his lips making me want to lean further over and kiss him.

I ignore the urge and say, "You do."

"Yeah, your mom is the best woman I know."

His words have me laughing and nostalgia rolls through me.

This used to be us.

Banter and jokes and having a good time.

I hope it's a good sign.

I hope Bran can forgive himself for all that's happened because the more time I spend with him, the more he opens up, the more I realize I don't need to. If I ever did.

My feelings for Bran have always been complicated. For a while he was like another younger brother, annoying as hell and one I had to compete with on the ice. Then somewhere around the time he hit his senior year of high school, something changed.

Maybe nothing really changed, maybe I just opened my eyes and saw him as more than a competitor. Saw him outside of being my brothers' friend. Somewhere in there, he became my friend.

His second year of college cemented our relationship. His struggle to cope with his mom's death sent him into a spiral and I was the closest in our family to his location.

Since I'd left home, it was the only time we had lived in the same city.

We spent more time together that year than we had the rest of our lives put together.

"Hey." Bran's hand lands on mine. "You okay?"

"Yes. Sorry. Just thinking."

"About what a great date you're on, I hope."

"Oh, this is a date? I thought—" His hand squeezing mine cuts me off.

"I said I wouldn't push and I won't. That was a joke. A bad one I guess."

"Not a bad one. And we can call it a date."

"You're going to be my boss. How does that work? Dating the boss?

"No clue. We don't have any rules about dating within the

org. It would be pretty hypocritical of us with Oakley and Walker."

"True. How—" He's interrupted by Marg delivering our drinks.

"Your food will be out in a minute. Can I get you anything else?"

"No. I'm good. Blake?"

"I'm good too. Thanks, Marg."

"You're welcome. Just holler if you think of something I can get you." Her words are accompanied by a look of yearning sent in Bran's direction.

"You really do have an admirer," I say when we're alone again.

"I don't know what to do about that. It's easy when she delivers the groceries. I pay her and shut the door."

"You do not shut the door in her face!"

"Not in her face..." He visibly cringes. "Okay, maybe in her face. *Shit.*"

Laughing, I reach for my iced tea and take a sip. "I'm sure she doesn't see it that way. Not with the way she's still looking at you."

"I've discovered I can't influence other people's minds."

"To a degree..."

"I know, my behavior toward them can affect what they think but really, is that in my control?"

"No. I guess not."

"And this conversation took a somber turn. Enough of that. Tell me about Oakley and Walker."

"Well, their story is one for the books, that's for sure."

"So tell me."

"We sent her to get his signature on a contract to coach the Rogues and instead she got his signature on a marriage certificate."

"Wait. They met and got married straight away?"

"No. Yes. Let me think... Two weeks? I think it was two weeks but that's not what the public believes."

"Oh?"

"We signed him to be the face of Rogue's new elite athlete line almost a year ago. Before his injuries. As far as the world knows they met then, and the friendship developed over time, culminating in their wedding last week."

"I don't know either of them very well, then or now, but what I do know makes me think they would be a good match."

"They are. You'll see for yourself when we head to Baton Rouge."

"I'm looking forward to it."

"First you'll get to see Mom and Dad."

"I'm looking forward to that too. Even if I've got some apologizing and explaining to do and I'm terrified they'll throw me off their property the second they lay eyes on me."

"They won't. And once you tell them, they'll understand."

"I don't need them to understand. I just need their forgiveness."

"I'm sure you'll get it."

"I guess we'll see."

"We will. And when I'm right, I'll be thrilled to say *I told you so*."

"You always were happy to shout from the rooftops when you won."

"Still am."

"Which roof did you shout from when you signed the contract for the Rogues?"

"Mine."

"Yours?"

"Yes. My house. In Baton Rouge. Then we all shouted from the top of the still under construction arena building."

"Fitting."

"We thought so."

"I think so too."

"Well, there will be more to shout about soon enough."

"Oh, like what?"

"Each time we sign a player."

"All of them?"

"Yes. Starting with you."

"I'm the first?"

"You will be."

BRANTON

I'm on the lake.

But it's different this time.

The trees are closer; stripped of leaves, they reach up to the sky with branches like bony hands, skeletal fingers grasping at the gray clouds hanging low above them.

It's not the lake. It's the pond.

I can hear blades slicing, grinding, racing. All sounds from my childhood.

The sky above me rumbles and a little girl giggles.

Laura?

When did Laura learn to giggle?

It's her. I know it's her.

Where is she? I can't see...there!

She's ahead of me, like always.

Except this time, she's not alone.

Her hands are held tight by two skaters I can't see, skaters who are taking her away...

"Laura!" I push hard, skate fast, yell loud. "Laura!"

It's no use. The quicker I go, the further they get in front of me. It's like I'm going in reverse. Except the trees are whizzing past in my peripheral and I know I'm moving forward because the other side of the pond is getting closer, the trees lining the bank bigger.

"Laura!"

My thighs cramp, ache with each push of my skates but I can't stop. Can't give up.

She needs me.

I'm the only one who loves her.

Stretching out a hand, I try to grab her. But I can't reach. She's too far.

"She doesn't belong to you anymore."

I stumble, the echoey voice floats around me as though coming from above.

Except I know it's not. It's from up ahead, next to Laura, and when her sweet laughter rings out across the ice, I know all my efforts are wasted.

I can't get to her.

I'll never reach her.

Never touch her.

Never be able to hold her again.

Should never have held her in the first place.

BLAKE

Shouting wakes me from a deep sleep.

At first I'm confused. The room unfamiliar, the bed not mine...

But then my brain shakes the cobwebs of sleep loose and I remember.

I'm in Parry Sound.

With Bran.

"Laura."

The cry has me throwing off the covers and launching out of bed. I know it's Bran even though the voice doesn't sound like his.

It's hoarse, raw, muted.

But it *has* to be Bran. There's no one else here.

Darting out of my room and into his, I don't understand what I'm seeing at first.

He's in bed, on his stomach across the middle of it, legs hanging off one side, arms reaching off the other.

"Laura!"

His arms stretch further, his fingers curl, release, curl, and his legs work like crazy. It's weird but I think he's trying to skate, trying to reach...

"Oh god."

He's having a nightmare about his daughter. Because this isn't a dream. He's not lost in some pleasant memory of his child. He's locked in the agonizing loss of his little girl. Real or imagined, the result is the same.

His grief is tearing him apart while he sleeps.

"Bran!" I race around the bed and reach for his shoulder. Giving him a shake, I yell, "Bran!" again.

He jolts but goes right back to pumping his legs, trying to grab onto something with his hands.

"Laura!"

I give him another shake, harder this time, but he's still trapped in the nightmare, his limbs still working, his breath huffing in and out of his lungs in harsh rasps. "Bran. Please. *Wake up*."

I hate seeing him like this. Hate that I can't help him, can't take away the pain he's obviously in. This time I grab his elbow, try to pull his arm down, but it's no use. He's too strong, too determined.

I'm just about to leave the room, pull an Oakley and dump a bucket of water over his head when he groans. The agony lacing the sound has my gut pinching, my heart stopping. There's another pained moan before he goes perfectly still, then his whole body sags, goes limp on the bed.

I don't know if the nightmare has let him go but I can't stand to watch him flail through it again so I move closer, close enough I can grip his head, tip it up and press my lips to his brow.

"Branton. Wake up. You have to wake up." My voice is a little above normal volume, my words stiff with command. "Wake. Up. Now."

"She doesn't belong to me anymore." His murmured words have my heart sinking, my lungs squeezing.

"Oh, Bran." I press a kiss to his skin. "I'm so sorry. So so sorry."

"I have to let her go."

My heart breaks for this man. I can't imagine, don't want to imagine, the agony of losing a child. Not in the circumstances Bran lost Laura. It was a tragedy and the fact it might have been avoided if he'd done anything different must weigh on him heavily.

It weighs on me and I've only just learned of what really happened.

What must it be like for him to live with that level of pain for years? Hell. He *hasn't* been living.

Has barely accepted my appearance in his hidey-hole. I thought the last couple of days have been better. He seems lighter somehow. I don't know if what I'm doing, pushing him to reclaim his life is the right thing. Maybe I should leave him be, let him find his way back on his own.

Except... I can't leave him like this. Now that I know what he's going through, what he's been through, I can't walk away.

Not like I did before.

And if I'd known then what I know now, I wouldn't have walked then either. I would have continued to call him, send him messages. More than the ones I did send. On his birthday. At Christmas.

Smoothing my hands over his head, I urge him to roll over. He's still asleep, muttering about letting Laura go, that he shouldn't have kept her this long, and I ache because I don't know what to do. How to help him.

Do I wake him up?

Do I leave him be now he's not calling out and thrashing around?

Do I curl up beside him and offer comfort, warmth, my presence, as reassurance he isn't alone?

With a sigh that seems to come from his toes, Bran rolls away, twists around, and reaches for a pillow. Pulling it beneath his head, he lets out another big breath and relaxes.

I watch him for a few minutes. Watch for signs the nightmare is back. Watch to see if his breathing is even. Watch because he's changed so much and yet he's still the same.

The same man I fell in love with. He's just laced with scars, hidden beneath barriers of his own making. I don't know if I'm strong enough to weather this with him.

I want to be.

I want to have a chance at the future we once talked about.

I want...

I want Branton Lattimer to be mine.

BRANTON

I'm on the lake.

But it's different this time.

The trees are closer; stripped of leaves, they reach up to the sky with branches like bony hands, skeletal fingers grasping at the gray clouds hanging low above them.

It's not the lake. It's the pond.

I can hear blades slicing, grinding, racing. All sounds from my childhood.

The sky above me rumbles and a little girl giggles.

Laura?

When did Laura learn to giggle?

It's her. I know it's her.

Where is she? I can't see...there!

She's ahead of me, like always.

Except this time, she's not alone.

Her hands are held tight by two skaters I can't see, skaters who are taking her away...

"Laura!" I push hard, skate fast, yell loud. "Laura!"

It's no use. The quicker I go, the further they get in front of me. It's like I'm going in reverse. Except the trees are whizzing past in my peripheral and I know I'm moving forward because the other side of the pond is getting closer, the trees lining the bank bigger.

"Laura!"

My thighs cramp, ache with each push of my skates but I can't stop. Can't give up.

She needs me.

I'm the only one who loves her.

Stretching out a hand, I try to grab her. But I can't reach. She's too far.

"She doesn't belong to you anymore."

I stumble, the echoey voice floats around me as though coming from above.

Except I know it's not. It's from up ahead, next to Laura, and when her sweet laughter rings out across the ice, I know all my efforts are wasted.

I can't get to her.

I'll never reach her.

Never touch her.

Never be able to hold her again.

Should never have held her in the first place.

Warmth surrounds me, a blanket of comfort I sink into. The swishing sound of the breeze fills my ears, ruffles my hair, and the restless sleep I just climbed out of falls away.

I'm tired. So tired. The heavy pull of oblivion, the quiet bliss of darkness swallows me, and I drift off into a sea of calm.

BLAKE

For the second night in a row, I'm out of bed and racing across the hall to Bran's room.

To his side.

It's the same as last night.

The same mad scrabble of legs, reaching arms and grabbing hands, shouts for Laura and murmurs of letting her go.

Once again, I'm able to soothe him or I've arrived as the nightmare releases its strangle hold. The ease with which he settles doesn't stop my heart from breaking to see him like this.

I wanted to ask him about it today, but he wasn't any different than he's been the whole time I've been here.

Which makes me wonder if I've missed the nightmares until now. If me being here is prompting them.

Does he know he's dreaming?

Does he know his grief is visiting him in his sleep?

Does he know he believes he has to let Laura go?

I don't know what he means by letting her go. Her memory? Because he never has to do that. He shouldn't even think he needs to do that.

Again I'm reminded of the lack of photos in the house, in his room. I've seen nothing. Not even a small snapshot of Laura.

It confuses me. When his mom died, he did everything he could to remind himself of her and one of those things was plastering every photo he could find on the walls of his apartment.

Did he do that here when he first arrived then remove them?

Could that be it?

Could he have once had her image surrounding him and recently taken them down, sending his healing backward?

I don't know how to ask. If I should ask. Is it even my place?

Sitting on the end of Bran's bed, I wait for his breathing to even out, go deep and relaxed, before getting to my feet. I leave him to sleep, like I did last night.

And like last night, I return to my room and toss and turn until just before dawn when I hear Bran stir, when he gets up and leaves his room to slip out the front door.

His morning ritual of watching the sun rise hasn't changed and while I haven't joined him a second time, I've lain in bed every day and listened.

BRANTON

I'm on the lake.

But it's different this time.

The trees are closer; stripped of leaves, they reach up to the sky with branches like bony hands, skeletal fingers grasping at the gray clouds hanging low above them.

It's not the lake. It's the pond.

I can hear blades slicing, grinding, racing. All sounds from my childhood.

The sky above me rumbles and a little girl giggles.

Laura?

When did Laura learn to giggle?

It's her. I know it's her.

Where is she? I can't see...there!

She's ahead of me, like always.

Except this time, she's not alone.

Her hands are held tight by two skaters I can't see, skaters who are taking her away...

"Laura!" I push hard, skate fast, yell loud. "Laura!"

It's no use. The quicker I go the further they get in front of me. It's like I'm going in reverse. Except the trees are whizzing past in my peripheral and I know I'm moving forward because the other side of the pond is getting closer, the trees lining the bank bigger.

"Laura!"

My thighs cramp, ache with each push of my skates but I can't stop. Can't give up.

She needs me.

I'm the only one who loves her.

Stretching out a hand, I try to grab her. But I can't reach. She's too far.

"She doesn't belong to you anymore."

I stumble, the echoey voice floats around me as though coming from above.

Except I know it's not. It's from up ahead, next to Laura, and when her sweet laughter rings out across the ice, I know all my efforts are wasted.

I can't get to her.

I'll never reach her.

Never touch her.

Never be able to hold her again.

Should never have held her in the first place.

I wake to the sensation of being watched—touched.

I know it's Blake. There's no menace behind the presence. Only a soothing calm.

I should let her know I'm awake, that I know she's here, but I don't want her to stop the gentle stroking of her fingers through my hair.

It's selfish. I obviously woken her up with my shouting. I must have done it last night and the night before too, although I didn't wake after those nightmares.

I know why bad dreams have begun plaguing me again.

I haven't had one since the day Blake arrived and now, with the looming need to tell her everything hanging over me, my subconscious is letting me know it's time.

If I leave it any longer, hide this last secret from her when I've already told her everything else...

Squeezing my eyes tight, I make a promise to myself.

I'll tell Blake the truth about Laura tomorrow.

And I'll accept whatever her reaction to the news is.

Even if she never wants to see me again.

BLAKE

I stifle another yawn and try to focus on the words in front of me.

Three hours of sleep are doing a number on my concentration. Not to mention my ability to keep my eyes open.

Last night after being woken by Bran having another nightmare, the third night in a row, I stayed in his room when he settled. I couldn't leave him alone like I had the two nights before.

I sat on the end of his bed and watched him sleep for a few hours, until he began to stir and the world outside the bedroom window began to lighten.

Only then did I slip back across the hall to my room where I lay there listening to him go through his morning routine.

I thought about joining him on the porch, but I wasn't sure if I could hold my tongue and I still don't know if I should bring up the dreams.

A message bubble pops up in the bottom right corner of my screen, drawing my attention.

OAKLEY

How's it going?

Good.

OAKLEY

He still interested?

He'd sign today if I put a contract in front of him. Without reading it.

OAKLEY

Wow. That's some voodoo charm you've got going on there.

No charm. Just history and a desire to get his life back.

OAKLEY

When will you be here?

At least another week. I want to head to Mom and Dad's for a while first. Take him with me.

OAKLEY

Let me know if you need anything. If he does.

Oh, and I'll pass on Branton's info to Drake. See if he's interested in taking on another client. Another Rogue.

Thanks. Tell Drake if he's interested, I'll get Bran to call when he's ready.

OAKLEY

Okay, talk later.

Staring at the screen, I think about Bran. About the trust he has in me. He's said it, and I know he means it—if I laid a contract in front of him, he'd sign on the dotted line without reading a word.

We used to have that level of trust. I'd thought it gone. Lost when he severed our relationship with a clean slice.

Now that I know what he's been through, what he had to deal with, I completely understand why he was there one minute, gone the next.

He wasn't just protecting me and the family, his friends, he was protecting himself—his unborn child. He might not see it that way, but I do. If he kept in contact, we would have had to meet Celeste and I think he knew on a subconscious level that would be a bigger mistake than the one he perceived himself making.

Noise behind me turns my head and I spot Bran coming in from the deck. "Nice walk?"

"Yeah. A little chilly this morning."

"Probably the cloud cover."

"Yeah, it's hovered for the last two days, keeping out the warmth of the sun."

"Will we get rain? Snow?"

"Not sure. But I checked the generator just in case we lose power."

"Is that something that happens a lot?" We haven't really talked about living here and while the weather probably isn't that different from where my parents live, Gannon Byrd's property butts up to the shoreline of Parry Sound.

"In winter a bit. But this place is set up for it. There's the wood pile to keep us warm if the power goes out. The generator runs basics like the refrigerator, but not the furnace, so good old fashion wood has the job of heating this place covered."

"Do we need to get more wood? I haven't noticed a wood pile."

"It's in the garage. Well, around the back of it." He moves to the fridge and opens it. "Are you hungry? Want me to make us something for lunch?"

"Around the back of the garage?"

"Huh." He glances over his shoulder. "Oh, yeah, the garage is split in two. Front section is for the car, the back is stocked with wood for the fire. Grilled cheese sound good?"

"Yes. Maybe some hot chocolate to go with it?"

"Sure. I can take care of both, you can keep working. I know being here doesn't mean you don't have work to do."

"More reading than anything. Making notes, questions about players to bring up at our next meeting. It'll be the first big one with Walker at the table."

"Want to share who you're looking at? I might be able to answer some questions."

"No. I'm good for now. Just narrowing down a list of players to begin with. More about their positions and stats at this stage."

"Well, let me know if I can help in any way."

"Making lunch is helping."

He gives me a smile, one that doesn't quite reach his eyes. "Sure. Give me ten and it'll be ready."

I don't know what the sad look is for. He's been doing it all morning so I know it's not because I just rejected his help. I haven't asked if there's something wrong because I'm frightened he's going to tell me to go. It's an irrational fear because he hasn't said anything about me leaving. Not even the day I arrived.

Hell, he sort of blackmailed me into staying for the week.

It has to be the lack of sleep messing with my head.

If Bran wanted me gone, he'd tell me. He's shown he's capable of shoving me out of his life already; I doubt he'd struggle to do it now.

"You want marshmallows with your chocolate?"

"Is there any other way to have it?"

"No. I just wasn't sure if you wanted it since we're having grilled cheese."

"I'll never pass up marshmallows with hot chocolate. It's the only way to drink it and yes that comes from experience. I have a supply of them to go with my chocolate at home. Never have one without the other in my house."

"Same." He reaches into the cupboard and pulls out two large mugs. "Want to eat outside or in here? Can you take a break from what you're doing?"

"I can. I'll grab a hoodie to put on. Unless you're going to turn the heaters on."

"You planning to go straight back to work after lunch?"

"Yes."

"Then grab the hoodie. I was going to get some washing done after lunch so I'll be inside too."

"Okay if I toss some of my stuff in the wash with yours?"

"How much have you got? I've let mine go a bit long so I have a least a full load."

"Only a couple of things."

"When you get the hoodie, drop what you have to wash off in my room and I'll put it together with mine."

"Thanks."

"No problem."

"Are the sandwiches smoking?"

"What— Shit!" Bran lunges for the stove and grabs the frypan. Moving it to the side he curses. "Fucking hell. Can't use that butter now."

"I don't mind it a bit brown." Mom used to make grilled cheese a light golden color but Dad always managed to burn the butter but somehow the sandwiches still tasted good.

"A bit brown yeah, black, no." He shakes his head,

frowning at the pan before huffing and bending to the cupboard where the pots and pans are kept. "I'm not even going to waste time cleaning it."

I watch him as he mutters about paying attention and slaps things around. First a glob of butter then the bread and cheese. I want to laugh. His antics are amusing but the look he gave me before is stuck in my head.

What has him sad?

Is it the dreams he's been having?

Maybe if the right opportunity arises, I can ask him about them over lunch.

BRANTON

Blake Watts has always had more faith in me than I ever had in myself.

Over the last few days, since the night we went into town for dinner, she's proven again and again my actions didn't shake that faith.

And if I could just snatch a little of it, believe in myself the way she does, I can use it to shore up my courage. Because it will take everything I have to do what I need to. I've put it off long enough.

The nightmares I've been having are proof of that.

If we're going to continue to build this relationship—the way we always should have—on and off the ice, there can't be any more secrets.

And I'm holding in a big one.

One I'm scared will ruin everything we've rebuilt since I woke to find her in my living room.

The same living room she's been working in for most of the day. I hate to disturb her, then again, that could be my shaky courage finding excuses not to do this.

Excuses like cleaning up our lunch dishes. Throwing two loads of laundry in the washer, switching them to the dryer. Sweeping the kitchen floor.

All cowardly bullshit I don't want to keep doing.

Snapping my spine straight and pulling back my shoulders the way her dad used to tell us showed we were confident—would make us *feel* confident—I move across the room until I'm beside her.

"Blake?"

"Hmm…" She's so engrossed in reading the files of possible Rogue players on her laptop she barely acknowledges me at first.

"Come for a walk with me?" I hold out my hand and wait for her to take it; the ease with which she slips her hand into mine brings a smile to my face.

Her faith, her trust, her support. She offers me all of them freely and even though I feel unworthy, I'm taking them.

Because after I tell her this final secret, I'll try my hardest to be the man she deserves if she'll still let me.

"Should I shut down my laptop?"

"No. We won't be gone long." Or she won't if she decides what I have to say is something she can't forgive.

"Where are we going?"

"Down to the water's edge. It's turned out to be a nice afternoon. I thought sitting in the sun and watching the water might be a nice break." I draw in a breath and force out the next words. "And there's something I need to tell you and I don't want to do it locked inside. I'd rather set this last skeleton free outside where it can be blown away by the breeze."

"That's rather poetic. And also a little scary. Is this about Celeste?"

"In a way, yes, but mainly it's about Laura."

"Then yes, Laura should be out in the fresh air, the sunshine."

My eyes meet hers. "How do you do that?"

"What?"

"Understand what I'm thinking before I do."

With a shrug she says, "I don't know. I've just always read your actions easily. I think it's why we've always been in sync. On and off the ice."

"I should never have shut you out."

"I'm not going to argue with that."

"It might have turned into a nice day, but it's still cool out, do you want to grab a coat? It might be colder by the water," I say as we move through the house.

"We've had the doors and windows open all afternoon, I think I'll be fine." She pauses by the door to the laundry room. "Should we put our boots on?"

"Are you planning to wade in?"

"No, are you?"

"No. The water is too cold this time of year and I've got something else in mind."

"The boulder to the north?"

There she goes again. Reading my mind. I wish I had the same ability when it comes to her, and I think at times I do. The one thing I definitely can't do is predict how she'll react to what I have to tell her.

That's a skill I'd give all my money to have right now.

"Yes. The boulder to the north is a great spot to sit and watch the water from. I've spent many spring days perched there gazing at the water, watching the breeze ripple the surface. It's a good thinking spot."

"I thought that the first time I saw it. Even imagined you there."

She smiles at me with the same love and affection I

remember from years past and I wish with everything in me I didn't have to do this, that I wasn't about to risk losing it again.

"If we're not wading, I'll stick with my runners."

"We'll keep to the tree line where the ground should be dry."

Decision made, we walk in silence as we leave the house and head into the trees. We're in the cooler shade for a few minutes before I begin to talk. I didn't plan to start this conversation until we reached our destination but now that I've made up my mind to tell her about Laura, I want it done.

And Blake's hand in mine, the muted light filtering through the branches above our heads, feels safe—right.

"I told you I didn't remember fucking Celeste."

"Yes. I remember."

"I don't remember it because I didn't do it."

"But—"

I give her hand a brief squeeze. "Let me get the whole story out, then you can ask questions, make comments."

"Okay."

"I don't remember talking to her at all, barely remember her being at the party that night, but the next morning I woke up with her in bed with me. Both of us were naked. I had no memory of getting there, no memory of taking off my clothes, so when she told me we spent the night together, I believed her. Although the disgust and disappointment in myself made me want to vomit as much as the idea of touching her, I *couldn't* argue. I didn't remember anything."

Taking a deep breath to steady the emotions from that morning, all the days since, bombarding me, I continue through the trees at a slow pace. Blake's hand in mine is a lifeline I need to get through the rest of the story.

"Three weeks later she showed up at my apartment with a positive pregnancy test and a request for money. I wanted to slam the door in her face the second I saw her. Wanted to give her whatever she asked for to make her go away so I could keep forgetting that morning like I'd forgotten the night before it, but then she said she just needed money to get rid of the baby and all I could think about was this defenseless baby—*my baby*—being ripped away and I couldn't let that happen."

Blake's hand tightens on mine. A silent expression of support and encouragement.

"The next few months were a living hell, some of which I've told you, and I think I knew before they handed me the baby that she wasn't mine to keep. That I'd only have her a short time. But I loved that little girl with everything in me."

"I would expect nothing less of you, Bran. No matter the circumstances."

"I loved her every minute of every day until the machines took her last breath. That day gutted me. Her loss devastating in a way I'd never experienced, wasn't sure I'd survive. But all of that pain was insignificant compared to what followed."

"Celeste's suicide."

"No. Her death brought me relief—peace—freedom. The note she left addressed to me shattered it. Shattered everything I'd believed and tore at what was left of my heart."

"What could she possibly have said that would be worse than losing Laura?"

"She was never mine to begin with. I never slept with Celeste. Never fathered her child. Laura isn't my biological child. Celeste just thought I'd be the easiest man to get money out of so she could get rid of her problem. As I read her words, my thoughts instantly went to Carl. They'd hooked up before and she'd tried again after she had Laura, but Carl isn't Laura's father either."

"Do you know who is?"

"Yes. No. It's complicated." We reach the water's edge and I lead her to the boulder and help her up before I say, "She told me in her note who but we'll never really know."

"Why would she tell you Laura wasn't yours then? After everything that had happened. She'd gotten everything she wanted out of you, leaving you that information to find after she was dead served no purpose."

"Didn't it? She spent our entire relationship threatening me, hurting me, blaming me for the situation she was in." I hold up a hand to stop the protest I see lurking in Blake's eyes. "It doesn't matter that none of it was my fault. She needed someone to blame and in spite of her actions it was never herself. I was the closest target, the easy target."

"I don't understand. Why you?"

"She pegged me for a sucker. She wasn't wrong. But she also chose me because I was close to the baby's real father."

"Who?"

"I need you to know that if I'd known before Celeste went off the rails and did what she did, hurt Laura, I would have said something, *done* something, made it right for Laura, for everyone."

"Of course. Why would I not think that?"

"I don't know who exactly fathered Laura—"

"But—"

"Did you know identical twins can have the same DNA?"

"No, but I guess it should be obvious if they're identical."

"Even science can't determine the father if identical twins sleep with the same woman and she gets pregnant."

"I'm enjoying this science lesson but what does—"

"The twins slept with Celeste."

"The twins?"

"Corbin and Landon."

"My brothers?"

"Yes."

"The twins?"

"Yes."

"But that means..."

"Yes."

"Oh god." One hand shoots up to cover her mouth, her eyes widen, instantly filling with tears, and she presses her other hand to her stomach as she leans forward. "Oh god, oh god, oh god."

I don't know whether to pull her into my arms and hold her or leave her be as she continues to chant 'oh god' and rock back and forth.

In the end, the tears sliding down her face leave me with no choice.

I can't *not* hold her.

BLAKE

The cold pressing against my cheeks barely registers. I went numb hours ago when Bran revealed the worst of his relationship with Celeste.

All I can think is I had a niece I never knew about, never saw, never held.

Laura.

"Did you choose her name?" My voice is hoarse, rough from all the tears I've shed.

"Yes."

"What did that cost you?"

"A sixty-thousand-dollar engagement ring."

Bran's words are flat, lifeless, and I can relate. It's how I feel right now. Gutted. I'm sure once the shock wears off, I'll be full of anger and resentment, frustration and disappointment, and most of all sorrow.

I can only image how Bran felt when he learned the girl he adored, thought was his, wasn't only gone, she'd never been his to begin with.

"You put yourself through so much only to find out she wasn't yours."

"She was. Maybe not by blood, but the second I agreed to pay Celeste to have the baby, to marry me, Laura was mine in every way that matters."

"You said that before. I didn't put it together then."

"I had her last name changed. After her death. I had them add Watts. Laura Jean Lattimer Watts."

"Oh, Bran." This man. So sure he's the villain in this whole drama when he's really the hero. "You have depths you don't give yourself credit for."

"It felt like the right thing to do. I haven't told anyone else. You and I are the only living people who know the truth."

"Do you want it to stay that way?" I want to tell my brothers, my parents, but it's not my decision to make.

"Yes. But should it? Don't your brothers, your parents, have a right to know?"

"I don't know what the right thing to do is. And I'm struggling to get past the fact I have a niece and I never got to meet her. Hold her."

"I was going to introduce her to the family after the divorce."

"We would have loved getting to see you again. Loved meeting her."

"I'm sorry I didn't tell you the other day. When I explained about Celeste. But talking about Laura..."

I lean to the side and rest my head on his shoulder. "I get it. Why you kept this last skeleton until now."

"If I tell them...I don't think I can do it on my own, without you there. I want you there."

The thought of telling my brothers cramps my stomach, churns until I think I might be sick. They were so vocal about

Bran's supposed betrayal I can't imagine either of them will take the news about Laura well.

"If you decide to tell them, I think you need to tell Mom and Dad first. They'll know how to handle the twins."

"I don't want to cloud the excitement surrounding the Rogues with this."

"It won't. For a start, this news is not for public consumption, and I'm not sure my parents will even agree with telling Corbin and Landon."

"I'll defer to them on this. If we tell anyone at all."

"I think you need to tell them, the twins. But it's up to you. It's just, I think this secret is part of the reason you're still living up here, hiding away, refusing to face another hard situation no one has a hope of winning."

"You're right. No one in this situation comes out on top."

"Okay. So you tell my parents and get their advice on telling the twins."

"I have to be honest, part of me wants to keep quiet, not mention Laura, not even think about Celeste, but I know that's to protect myself. To keep her mine a little longer."

"Keeping it all bottled up doesn't help you, Bran. It just festers and turns more poisonous. I think your instinct to come out here, in the sunshine, the fresh air, to tell me you weren't Laura's biological father was spot on. She deserves to be in the light. And people, *her* people, need to know about her. I get why you want to keep her for yourself, but she deserves to be shared."

"I should never have cut you all off. If I hadn't, Celeste might have told me sooner, Laura might not be gone."

"There's no point playing what if. So many things could have been different. If Celeste had gone to either of my brothers, they would have stepped up. I don't understand why she didn't."

"I don't think she wanted to. She didn't want the baby. I spent months making sure she ate right, took her vitamins, got enough sleep. I had to search the house regularly for alcohol, dump it down the drain when I found it. I think she thought I'd just give her money."

"You did."

"But it came with conditions. She had to have the baby. Marry me so I had some control over the situation. I went to every doctor's appointment I could, something else she bitched about all the time."

"She picked the wrong guy for a quick fix."

"She picked the wrong guys to sleep with too. Corbin or Landon, whoever she chose to tell, would have pushed for the same as me. To be honest, I didn't believe Laura could be theirs at first but when I thought about it, when I looked at the million and one pictures I took of her in those short weeks, she has the twins' eyes. Your eyes."

"She does?" I want to ask to see, except I don't think I'm ready for that. Maybe in a few hours—tomorrow.

"I'll show you when we go back to the house."

"I understand why you hate Celeste."

"I don't hate her. I *despise* her. The trauma she inflicted, on me, on her daughter, it was cruel, and I will never forgive her. I'm glad she's dead. If she wasn't, I don't know if I could stop myself from strangling the life out of her. I'd gladly do the time for it."

"I'd come visit you. Then again, with what I know now, I'd probably be in my own cell."

"I don't want to ask, but I have to. Are we okay? Does this ruin what we've started here?"

"What? No!" I tip my head back to look at him. "Of course not. Why would you even think that?"

"I've lied to you so many times."

"Have you? From where I stand, it looks more like keeping information from me. That's not lying. Not in my book. And you did it to protect Laura, to protect me, from Celeste, yourself from more pain. I see that. I didn't at first, I do now."

"I don't intend to keep you in the dark ever again. Or lie. I know we haven't really talked about us as a couple but you have to know, that's what I want. I'm prepared to wait as long as you need to."

"You don't think we've waited long enough?"

"Yes. But I don't want to rush things, fuck anything up, and we have unfinished business to deal with, then the Rogues to get off the ground."

"Oh, we do, do we?"

"Yes, we do. I told you I'd sign. I meant it."

"Then you should probably get yourself a new agent."

"Know any good ones?"

"Actually, yes, Walker's agent, Drake. He's a shark at negotiating but also fair. He won't bullshit you and he'll go to bat for you to get a better deal."

"The one you're offering isn't good?"

"Oh, it's good. On par with what you had before."

"I'd play for free."

"You don't need to do that, and you shouldn't. Your talent and the hard work you put into honing your skills is worth something."

"I guess."

"There's no guessing. Just because you do something you love doesn't mean you shouldn't get paid for it."

"I'm not sure I love it like I used to."

"Why the hell not? There was nothing wrong with your game before…"

"No, but it's the game that led me down the path I ended up on." His gaze meets mine, his eyes a maelstrom of swirling emotions. "If I hadn't been so single focused on getting signed to an NHL team, I would have gotten on my knees and begged you to marry me. I never would have met Celeste. Never would have married a woman I didn't like, never mind love."

"And you wouldn't have had Laura."

"Sometimes I wonder if those five and half weeks with her were worth it."

"Don't say that. Don't ever say that. You loved her. *Love* her. She knew that, I know it because I know you love me."

"I do. I never stopped. Could never stop and I'm scared shitless if I come out of hiding, if I join the Rogues, my past is going to come roaring back and ruin everything all over again."

"You survived it once, you can survive it again."

"Did I though?" He waves a hand at the trees behind us. "I've been hiding in the woods for two years, refusing to answer the phone or talk to anyone I didn't have to."

"But you didn't want to."

"What?"

"You didn't want to leave here. Now you do."

"And?"

"Wanting to come out of hiding makes all the difference. If you didn't want to, you wouldn't put in the effort you have with me the last few days, you wouldn't be talking about playing for the Rogues, going to Mom and Dad's. You'd be telling me to leave and pushing me down the driveway."

"I'll never push you away again."

"Well, here's the deal, Branton Lattimer. I don't want to live hidden away in the woods. I want to live every minute of every day and make the Rogues a success. So if you want to be with me, if you're serious about us as a couple, you have to leave your safe place and find a new one. One that lets you live."

"That's you."

"What?"

"You. *You're* my safe place. I barely got through the day before you turned up in my living room. Now I'm bounding out of bed each morning ready to hang out, go for a hike, explore Parry Sound. Whatever you want to do, I want to do. Without you, none of that enthusiasm exists. You're my reason for living."

BRANTON

Seven days.

So much has changed in a week.

Last week I was in Parry Sound willingly spending my days alone with no inclination to leave. And now, my bags are packed and in the back of a rented SUV heading down the highway, Blake in the passenger seat beside me as we drive toward her parents' place.

After our talk yesterday, Blake said we weren't waiting any longer to get my life back. She'd had enough of letting me decide when we left Gannon's place. She was taking charge.

I don't know how she did it, but when we woke this morning there was a car in the driveway, keys under the front door mat, and after packing up and locking down the house, we were on the road, our route plotted, less than three hours later.

That was two hours ago.

"You want to stop for lunch or keep going?" I ask as a sign for the next exit flies by.

"If we keep going, we'll get to Mom and Dad's well before

dinner." Twisting around, she reaches into the backseat and comes back with a bag of trail mix. "I've got this to keep us going but maybe we can swing through a drive thru somewhere and get food to eat along the way. If you're hungry."

"I'm not hungry. The bacon and egg sandwiches you made us before we left the house are still clinging to my ribs." Blake packed them to go, and I ate three and a half of them in the first fifteen minutes of our journey. This new life I'm going after has me ravenous but once again, Blake came through for me.

"Me too. And I ate less than you."

"Half of one doesn't really count as less."

"Of course it does. Besides, when I talked to Mom last night, she said Dad would be grilling steaks on the barbecue for dinner tonight and we were welcome to share if we didn't dawdle."

The mention of her parents has my stomach clenching. I can't wait to see them. It's been years, and excitement at seeing the two people who mean as much to me as my own mother fills my chest.

Except I can't deny the layer of trepidation that has a choke hold on my heart.

I let them down.

I let everyone down.

If my mom was alive, she'd slap me upside the head and call me a dumbass for the way I behaved. The only saving grace of losing Mom is she didn't get to witness the biggest mistake of my life unfold.

"So, steak dinner or lunch?"

"That's not a question. Steak. One hundred percent steak, every time. Breakfast, lunch, and dinner if it's an option."

Laughing, Blake tears open the bag of trail mix. "Hold out your hand."

When I do as asked, she tips a small pile of nuts and dried fruit into my palm. "No cranberries?"

"No. I'm still in the habit of buying our preferred brand."

"Thanks."

"For what, liking the same thing as you?"

"No. For not wiping me from your life when I wiped you from mine."

"Did you wipe me? You never thought about me? Never wished things were different?"

"I tried not to. Every damn day. Couldn't seem to do it most of the time."

"Then we're even."

"We'll never be even."

"Agree to disagree."

"I won't let you down like I did before."

"I think you let yourself down when you cut us out more than anyone else, Bran."

Blake's phone rings before I can argue. I expect her to take the call; what I don't expect is for her to grin and put it on speaker. "Hello... Drake."

Her drawn-out greeting has me smiling.

"Blake. I'm told you have a new client for me."

I don't recognize Drake's voice but I know who he is, and his words have me glancing at Blake.

"I do. He's right here and I have you on speaker."

"I can't talk to him with you listening."

"Why not?"

"Two words. Conflict. Interest."

"Oh, come on. I know you read through Walker's contract in front of Oakley."

"I did. But we didn't *talk* about it in front of Oakley."

"Fine. I'll stick my fingers in my ears."

"Very funny. Branton, I assume you can hear me."

Their back and forth has me grinning even though they're talking like I'm not here. "Yes."

"Good. I'd be happy to take you on so get my number from Blake and when you've got a minute, give me a call. And when you do, leave her in another room."

"Drake!"

"Listen, Watts, I want you guys to succeed as much as you do but I'm not letting you do it on the backs of my clients."

"He's not your client yet."

"I believe I just said he was."

"I don't see a signed contract. Send it to me and I'll pass it on to Bran. After I've looked at it."

"Blake, I love you and your girls, but we're doing this right. I don't need another Walker and Oakley media fiasco."

"Ah...well..."

"Shit. I don't want to know. Whatever is going on keep it out of the spotlight until after we get Branton squared away."

"We're heading to my parents' place for a few days then we'll be going to Baton Rouge. Together."

"Say hello to your dad for me. And give me a heads up before you leave Canada. Does Nat know what your movements are?"

"For an agent to some players, you're sounding awfully invested in the Rogues management."

"I've got my top client signed on as head coach, the guy who you've all referred to as your Hot Shot is my new client, Nat mentioned a wonder kid she wants me to look at—"

"Since when are you and Nat buddy-buddy?"

"Since I helped defuse the Cantrell disaster."

"From what I hear, the Cantrell disaster isn't over yet and only getting bigger."

"Yeah." Drake's sigh comes through loud and clear, makes me curious to know what they're talking about. "Laken held another press conference yesterday. Once again, she stressed Jerry does not own, nor is he involved in any way with the Knights org. According to her, he doesn't even have season tickets."

"Good for her. Although I assume Jerry's still throwing his weight around like he *does* own the place if she's holding yet another conference."

"Yes, unfortunately."

"I would have thought he'd lay low after the Kristina debacle. Surely her illegal activities and charges make him cautious."

"You wouldn't be alone in thinking that, but this is Jerry. He's always had an overinflated opinion of himself."

"He has. I'm glad Laken has decided to put him in his place."

"I don't think she had a choice. It was either that or have the NHL hand out fines, and there was talk of a points penalty, deducting them from the team, which would drop them out of playoff contention."

"Oh. Harsh."

"Jerry leaked information on the Rogues franchise, info he shouldn't have had. The NHL had to do something about it."

"I get that. But what can they do now? Jerry isn't associated with the Knights other than being married to the owner and the son of the previous owner."

"Wait. Jerry is Gerald Junior?" I interrupt, my brain finally connecting the dots and working out who they're talking about.

"Yes, the pompous ass decided after his father died that he didn't need to be a junior anymore. Made everyone call him Jerry or Mr. Cantrell," Blake explains. "I'll tell you the rest later but the short of it is Gerald Senior left the team to Laken, not Jerry."

I glance at Blake before returning my eyes to the road. "Wow, that must have chapped Junior's ass."

"Apparently he didn't know about it until a few weeks ago. Right around—"

"I'd love to keep chatting with the two of you, but I've got a call I need to make," Drake interrupts. "Speaking of calls, I'll be waiting for yours, Branton. Talk later, Blake."

"Okay. I'll let you know when we head home."

"Thanks. Bye."

We're quiet for a few moments after Drake hangs up. It gives me time to think about his call. The fact Blake wasn't surprised to get it.

"Did you tell him about me?"

"No. Nat did. Or Oakley. I can't remember. We've spoken to him about a couple of his current clients. He's joked about becoming the Rogues in-house agent because he reps more than a few of the players we're looking at."

"And you want me with him too?"

"No. I want you with someone I trust. Someone that won't dump you when shit hits the fan."

"In all fairness, Mal didn't really have a choice. I'm sure if I called him, he'd take me on again."

"No. Not happening. I told you when you signed with him, he wasn't the best fit and he proved that when he didn't look out for you when everything happened."

"Mal's a good guy. He did his best."

"If that was his best, I'd hate to see his worst."

"I'm not sure anyone could have dealt with the fallout of my tailspin any better."

"Drake would have. It's why I'm going to tell you to sign with him. He's got one of the best reputations and he's proven himself over the last few weeks with the situation surrounding the Rogues franchise leak, and Walker and Oakley getting together, as well as Walker signing on as our head coach."

"I can see how that might be a bit of a scandal." And if I get my wish, if Blake and I become a couple, our situation will be the same. I'll be sleeping with my boss.

"The deal with Walker's ex and Cantrell was just as scandalous but as usual, the press likes to tear down a successful woman more than exposing a deceitful man."

BLAKE

The closer we get to Mom and Dad's, the more nervous Bran becomes. There're no obvious signs, no bouncing knee or tapping fingers. It's the clench of his fingers on the wheel, the tautness of his body in the seat. And the heavy feel of the air around us.

"It's going to be fine. They don't hate you, could never hate you," I murmur into the thick air.

One thing I know about my parents is they would never judge someone for mistakes made with the best intentions. They love each of us kids, and that includes Bran, with their whole hearts—unconditionally.

"I have a lot to explain, apologize for. Looking back, knowing how things ended up, I'm not sure I'd have done anything differently with regard to Celeste and Laura. It's cutting them out of my life I need them to understand and forgive me for."

"They will." I know it as well as I know my own name. "Do you want another water?"

"No. If I drink another drop we'll have to pull over."

"You need to pee? Because I'm up for a quick bathroom break if you are." My own bladder has been full for over an hour but I didn't want to delay our arrival when Bran is having a hard time with it.

"Why didn't you say so?" Bran's eyes land on mine for a second before returning to the road. With a frown on his face, he mutters, "I'm already failing."

"Already failing? Failing what?"

"Taking care of you. I should have realized you needed to go the same as me. You're smaller and we've both finish two water bottles since we started the drive."

"I can take care of myself, and like you, I thought getting to Mom and Dad's quicker was the better choice. Especially after we got held up by the road works."

"Well, it's not. That last sign said there's a gas station up ahead, off the next exit. We can fill up the tank while we're there."

"You know I could argue that you need to take care of you as much as me. I need you—the Rogues need you—in peak form. Holding on to a full bladder until it bursts is not a healthy decision."

"It's not that full. I was exaggerating."

"Still, we're ahead of time because we didn't stop for lunch and the roadworks didn't really hold us up that long. If you needed to go, we could have taken a ten-minute bathroom break."

"Well, we are now."

Bran changes lanes and a few minutes up the road, he takes the exit. The gas station is another few minutes of driving and my estimated ten-minute break is looking short. But like I said, in spite of the delays, we're on track to get home before Dad will be slapping the steaks on the grill.

"Where will I live when we get to Baton Rouge?"

Bran's question has me turning to face him. "Where do you want to live?"

"I have options?"

"Yes. We have a complex of townhouses and apartments. Most of those are empty at the moment, but they'll fill up quickly now that some of the arena is open and the Rogue sportswear head office is being fitted out."

"Where do you live?"

"In a house. I bought it when we first looked at relocating and going after the franchise. It's not huge but there's enough room for you to stay until you get an idea of where you want to be."

"With you."

"With me? You want to stay with me until you decide?"

"No. I want to stay with you forever."

He's talked about being a couple and I think we've gotten our friendship close to what it was before he broke off contact, but I don't know if I'm ready to dive into a more intimate relationship yet. "Bran."

"If you don't want me to stay with you, that's fine. I'll take whatever, wherever."

"That's not what I meant. I'm okay with you staying in my house. But I'm not ready to commit to the forever you keep talking about."

"I know. I'm sorry. I'm pushing." His gaze meets mine for a split second before he returns his attention to the turn into the gas station. "I've been dead inside—no, not dead, in pain, aching, for so long that now it's not as sharp, almost dull like a fading memory, I want to grab the life I let go, the life I shoved aside, with two fists and hold on."

The emotion in his voice is raw, it slices at my insides as sharply as a razor blade. I want to soothe him, tell him he can have what he wants, but I need to take this—us—slow. I'm okay going all in on him playing for the Rogues but when it comes to my heart, to handing it over to him, I can't yet. He has it. There's no doubt about that, but I'm not ready for him to hold it freely.

Mainly because while he's saying all the right words, he's still got a lot he needs to work through. A lot of people to talk to and make amends with.

"How about we worry about that when we get to Baton Rouge. I plan to be at Mom and Dad's for a week. I want to run you through your paces with Dad's expert eyes as a second set. That will give us time for you to settle in to life outside of your hidey-hole and for you to make steps toward mending some fences."

Bran pulls up to a pump and shuts off the engine. Turning in his seat, he rests one arm on the steering wheel and reaches the other toward me. I give him my hand, our fingers seamlessly weaving together.

"I can do whatever you need me to do. What I can't do is face any of that without you by my side. I meant what I said the other day. You are my safe place. I need you with me. Want you with me."

"I can be there as much as you need or want for now but once we get to Baton Rouge, I'll have other things I have to do. Like my job. Actually, I have several roles within Rogue sportswear and the Rogues org but the main one is getting the roster for the team filled out."

"I can help with that."

"How?"

"It might have been a couple of years, but I've played with or against a lot of players, I know the sport, I can be your sounding board, and I've probably got some inside info on a few of the players on your list that could tip your decision to offer them a contract one way or the other."

Smiling, I say, "My own personal advisor?"

"Yes."

"As long as it doesn't interfere with your training, I don't see a problem with it."

"Good. Now go pee while I top up the tank." He pops the driver's door and slips out before I can mention his own need of the bathroom.

Not that he needs me to mother him. He might have looked like he needed taking care of when we first arrived in Parry Sound, but it couldn't be further from the truth.

Branton Lattimer is a big boy, literally and figuratively. He can take care of his own needs. And I need to remember that.

Getting out of the car, I grab my phone and make a call as I head to the bathroom.

Mom answers on the second ring. "How close are you now?"

With a laugh I shove the bathroom door open and lock it behind me. "About an hour, depending on traffic. We're just stopping for gas."

"Don't forget to go to the restroom before you leave."

"Always a mom."

"Of course. I've told you before, being a parent is a lifetime job."

"You have. I believe you. I just wonder if it's really necessary to tell your thirty-one year old daughter to go use the washroom before a car ride."

"Old habits die hard. Plus I still need to remind your brothers to go. Especially the twins."

The mention of Corbin and Landon has me wishing I'd sent a text instead of calling. It's hard to act normal with the secret Bran shared weighing on my mind. "How are those two? Still talking trash about my team?"

"I haven't spoken to either of them since our video call the other week." She's silent for a moment before she asks, "Is everything all right?"

"Yes. It's fine. Bran's a little tense. Worried about how you and Dad will react when we get there." I hope the small nugget of information will keep her happy. She can dig in deep once we arrive at the house.

"The only thing he needs to worry about is whether your father will break any of his ribs when he crushes him in a hug."

"Dad's okay with him coming?"

"What kind of question is that? Branton is like a son to us. Of course we're happy, and I've had to hide the car keys for the last week so your dad didn't slip away and drive to where you were. He wants Branton back where he belongs."

I love my parents. And their unconditional love of their children, of Bran, is only one of the reasons. "I love you. Tell Dad I love him too and we'll see you both in about an hour."

"Will do. Drive safe. And tell Branton we love him as much as we love you."

"Okay. See you soon."

After I hang up, I don't waste time taking care of business. I'm eager to get back on the road so I can get one of those crushing hugs from my dad Mom spoke about.

As I leave the bathroom, I run into Bran. Literally. Bounce right off his hard body and hit the wall behind me.

"Shit. Sorry." His hands wrap around my upper arms and steady me. "I didn't expect you to come out of there like a pilot in an ejection seat."

"My fault. I talked to Mom before I used the bathroom and now I can't wait to get home. I need a hug from Dad."

"Everyone needs a hug from Andrew Watts at least once in their life." A sad smile lifts his mouth on one side. "I wish Laura had gotten the chance to do that."

BRANTON

I remember being so nervous I thought I'd pee my pants the first time I drove through the gates of the Watts home. If I hadn't emptied my bladder an hour ago I'm sure I'd feel the urge to go now too.

Mom was at the wheel all those years ago. I was 6 years old, had just lost my father, and she was driving us to what she called our 'fresh start'.

I didn't understand it back then. It wasn't until I was older, a teenager, that I understood what she meant. I get it now even more.

We never talked about it but she had to have been so excited—so scared. To uproot us from the only home I'd ever known and move us clear across the country after such a terrible loss.

The job of live-in housekeeper and occasional babysitter the Watts family had offered her must have seemed like a miracle to a woman who hadn't worked outside the home in years.

They'd given us a safe place to stay, given us a family to love —be loved by—and introduced me to the first love of my life.

Hockey.

It had taken another eight years for me to find my second love and for years I lived with the knowledge I'd never have her.

I was nineteen when Blake finally noticed me the way I noticed her. Six years my senior, I figured the attraction on her side would be fleeting, would fizzle out.

Except Mom died and I'd floundered in my grief until I was at the point of flunking out of class and losing my spot on my college hockey team.

Blake had turned up on my doorstep and stuck with me, pushing and pulling, and dragging me back to the man-boy I'd been before Mom's death. Those months formed a bond that even Celeste couldn't break.

It's damaged but still there. Still tethering us together the way we'd been before I let myself be hoodwinked by a lying bitch.

And I hate that I have to bring Celeste here, even if it is only in memory. I don't want her tainting this place. The sanctuary of my youth, the birthplace of my future.

"It's going to be okay."

I glance over at Blake. "You sound so sure."

"I am."

"I'm not."

"I know. Just remember that no matter what, we all love you."

"The twins made it pretty clear after I married Celeste, the emotion they felt for me was the opposite side of the love coin."

"Yeah, well, they never did learn to keep their opinions to themselves, well Landon mostly. Corbin seems to know when to keep his mouth shut. Sometimes. And as much as I hate to say it, I think finding out about Laura may change that. Change them."

"We haven't decided to tell them yet. We need to tell your parents first."

"One would argue Laura's parent should know before her grandparents."

"But we don't know which one of them is her father. And it's unlikely a DNA test would shed any light on the subject. Not if they carry near identical DNA themselves."

"I guess they get to share Laura like they've shared everything else in their lives."

The driveway is long, weaving through trees before the property opens up to reveal the house. When we break through that shelter I can see two people standing at the bottom of the front stairs.

"We have a welcoming committee."

"The security system would have alerted them when we opened the gate."

"I remember."

"May as well park near the front door. They'll only follow us to the garage if you don't."

"Less of a hike to carry our bags too."

"I'm not the one with more than one bag to carry."

"I don't understand how you have so much packed into that duffel bag. I took bare essentials when I left the house in New York and I still needed two large suitcases and a duffel."

"I'm used to traveling light. Until I quit skating, hell, even when I coached the Canadian Women's team, I didn't have a home base. Just lived out of two bags. The rest of my stuff was here. Not that I had much."

"And your house in Baton Rouge?"

"Don't worry. Once I put down roots, I fitted the place out with everything."

"Practice rink?"

"Except that. I thought about it, but the basement is small and a rink that size wouldn't do much for a toddler, never mind an adult."

"I guess now that the Rogues practice facility is open, you can use that."

"Every day. And I'll be dragging your ass there with me. There will be no slacking off on my watch."

"Noted."

Through the windshield I see Andrew Watts staring at me like he wants to drill a hole in my head. Easing the car to a stop beside the front stairs, I've barely moved the gear shift into park when Blake unbuckles her belt, flings the door open and bounds out.

I smile when she does the same thing she'd done as long as I've known her. Running straight at her dad, she launches into the air a good six feet from him. And like every other time I've watched them do this, he catches her and spins in a circle.

Taking a deep breath, I switch off the engine and climb out of the SUV at a more sedate pace. By the time I reach the hood, Blake has moved on to her mom, the two of them wrapped in each other's arms.

Forcing myself to move closer, I head for Andrew first. Putting out my hand, I smile. "Hey, good to see you, Mr. Watts."

"What is this Mr. Watts bullshit? And since when do we shake hands, son?" In spite of his words, his hand grips mine. With a quick yank, he pulls me in, saying, "Come here, dumbass, this is how we say hello."

I find myself in an embrace worthy of an Olympic medal if hugging was a sport. Blake and I talked about Andrew's hugs earlier. How everyone should be the recipient of one at least once in their lifetime.

Maybe it's the welcome. Maybe it's the reality of Laura never meeting this amazing man. Or maybe it's the walls I've hidden behind for years finally crumbling to dust. Whatever it is, like hugging Blake a week ago, emotions I've bottled up come flooding out.

The big man doesn't even flinch. Just holds me tighter. Lets me lose myself in the body-wracking sobs tearing through my chest.

"I've got you, son. Let it out."

Andrew's words, spoken softly in my ear, seem to give freedom to more of the pain I've let fester and eat away at me.

I didn't cry this hard after Laura took her last breath. Not when I saw the teeny coffin they'd put her in. Not when I found out not only didn't I get to keep her, she hadn't been mine to keep in the first place.

I vaguely hear Blake and her mom head inside. But the pain and the tears don't stop. No matter how hard I try to hold them back, how hard I want to stand on my own, neither of those things happen.

The sobs ease a little and Andrew says, "A good purge does wonders for the soul. Now let's head inside. There's a couple of ice cold beers waiting for us by the grill along with some juicy fat steaks we need to cook."

I'm a snotty mess when I pull back and Andrew does the damnedest thing. He pulls the hem of his shirt up and wipes my face like I'm a toddler with a runny nose.

I have no words. No idea how to thank this man for everything he's done for me in my life. I shut him out, cut him off without a word of explanation and the first time he sees me in years, he's pulling me in, offering me comfort and support as though the last time we spoke was yesterday.

"I'm sorry." It's not enough, I know it, he has to know it.

"For what? Going off and living your life?"

"For cutting you out of it. For the things I have to tell you. For hurting Blake."

"That last one I'll take the apology for. The rest, I'm sure isn't of your making."

"How can you know that?"

"Because I might not be your father but I'm the closest damn thing to it you've had for most of your life. I watched you grow up, *helped* you grow up. The boy I raised would never hurt the people he loves intentionally. I know you have reasons. Reasons I'm probably going to get pissed off about. But, Branton, you are mine as much as the four boys and girl my wife saw fit to grace me with."

"I—"

He claps me on the shoulder and steers me toward the house. "Let's get that beer. And throw those steaks I've been marinating all day with special smoky barbecue sauce on the grill."

"Mom's secret recipe?"

"Is there any other? I'd never be caught dead using anything else."

"I haven't mastered her sauce. Tried but no luck. Her stew though, I've got that pretty close in recent years."

"You'll have to make us a batch while you're here. Any idea how long that will be?" He pushes the front door open and leads the way in. "I miss my girl more now she lives on the same continent than I did when she was traipsing around the world searching for gold."

"Blake said a week. She wants to run me through my paces with you watching. I've kept in shape but haven't played a game with anyone since..."

"No worries about that. It's like riding a bike. I might see if any of the boys have free time to head out here. We might get ourselves a pickup game like we did when you were all little."

"I need to talk to you before you do that." I swallow through my tight throat. "I have some things to tell you, advice to ask, before I can see anyone else."

"Okay. We'll have a couple of beers, eat a couple of juicy steaks, and then if you're up to it we can take a walk out to the pond."

"I'd like that, but I want Blake with me, and Mrs. Watts needs to hear what I have to say too."

"As much as I want to tell you to spill it now, I think we'll all do better with whatever you have to share if our bellies are full."

"It might be better to hear this on an empty stomach. Nothing to throw up then."

"Branton, you are not making me feel better about waiting."

"Sorry. I'm projecting. I'm the one who's likely to throw up."

"No throwing up in my house, Branton Lattimer." Larissa Watts slips her arm around my waist for a side hug. "Now when will the steaks be ready? I've got loaded potatoes ready to bake but they're best served hot out of the oven."

"Give us ten, then put them in. That will give us time to crack a second beer." Andrew grins.

"Might be best to pass on the second beer. I'm opening a bottle of red to go with dinner."

"Oh, we're bringing out the good stuff?"

"Always do when one of my babies comes home. And tonight I've got two of them under my roof."

BLAKE

Bran has barely touched his dinner. He's sampled everything but nothing more than a bite or two of each has passed his lips.

Leaning over I whisper, "Not hungry?"

"No." The look he gives me makes me want to wrap my arms around him and tell him it'll be okay. And while I believe that, I'm sure things are going to be rocky before they're okay.

"Should I put that in the fridge for you, Branton?" Mom asks. "In case you get hungry later."

"I... Yes, but I can do it." He pushes back from the table and picks up his plate. "Can I clear anyone else's?"

"We'll do it later. Why don't you grab that second bottle of wine off the counter on your way back? I think another glass for everyone might get us through the next few minutes." Mom's smile is small, a gentle curve of her lips, and her eyes are full of worry, compassion.

I want to wrap my arms around her too. I want to protect the big man next to her as well.

If I could, I'd travel back in time and slap both my brothers upside the head. Knock some sense into them before they did a stupid thing and both fucked Celeste.

"Okay. I'll be right back."

When Bran is out of earshot, Dad leans over the table and asks, "How bad?"

Shrugging, I try to offer a smile but I know it falls short of being reassuring. "Bad-ish. And good."

"What kind of answer is that?"

"It's the one I've got."

"Okay, tell me, do I need to go out and take care of someone?"

"No. They—" Shaking my head, I rethink my words. I don't want to reveal anything. It's Bran's story to tell. "He needs you to listen and understand why he did what he did. And I need you to remember he removed himself from life the last few years to punish himself for what happened."

"I hid away because I'm a coward." Bran's voice has us all swinging around.

I have no idea how long he's been standing there and as much as I want to apologize for talking about him, I won't. I said nothing I wouldn't say in front of him. "You are not a coward."

"I agree. Sometimes things take a while for us to understand, to work out, and some things require a long time to do it."

"I appreciate the words, Larissa, but when it comes down to it, I was hiding so I wouldn't have to face this. And to keep what was never mine a little longer."

"I think you better sit down and explain." Dad indicates Bran's chair and holds out his hand. "Give me the wine, I'll pour while you talk."

Sitting beside me again, Bran reaches for my hand and grips it tight. "I woke after a party one weekend with Celeste in bed with me. I didn't remember the night before so when she said we slept together I had no choice but to believe her."

"You sound like you shouldn't have," Dad interrupts.

"I'm getting to that," Bran says as I say, "Let him talk."

Mom sends me a look, one that says she knows there's been a change in our relationship. "Please, ignore the man who lacks patience unless it's on the ice and go on, Branton."

"I put it out of my mind until she showed up at my place a few weeks later with a positive pregnancy test and a request for money. Money to *get rid of the problem*. As much as I wanted to hand over some cash and be done with Celeste, I couldn't do it."

"Of course not!"

Mom eyes Dad with the quelling look she used to give us as kids when she wanted us to be quiet or behave.

"Sorry. Go on."

I can't help but smile when Dad sits back and rests his hands in his lap. It won't last long. He's always been vocal and not afraid to speak his mind.

"Long story short, I convinced her to have the baby, to marry me. In hindsight it was probably the wrong thing to do but at the time I didn't see any other option. Things between us were not good. Actually, they were bad. Really bad. We fought all the time and when Laura was born, Celeste didn't want to do anything for her, didn't want anything to do with her."

Bran reaches for his glass and takes a few big gulps. Probably for courage and to stall, to shore himself up for what he needs to reveal next. Placing my free hand on the pair we have entwined, I give him an encouraging squeeze.

"I thought things would be okay because I'd talked Celeste into getting a divorce, to signing over parental rights, to leave Laura with me." He swallows another mouthful of wine. "She,

Celeste, tried to hook up with a guy she'd been with before. I don't know all the details but it didn't go well, and the comments must have been about her post-baby body because she came home yelling about me and Laura ruining her life, ruining *her*."

"Bitch." The muttered word comes from Mom and has all of us focusing on her. "What? I call it like I see it."

I hide my smirk and tighten my hold on Bran's hand.

"That night was bad. I'll give you the full details if you want but basically, Celeste hurt Laura and when I got her to the hospital, it was already too late. I'm not sure there was ever a chance... The next day, they, the doctors, told me she had no brain activity, the machines they had her connected to were the only things keeping her alive, and I needed to—" Bran chokes and Dad pushes from his seat and moves around behind him.

"I think I'm going to hold you through the rest of this." Dad doesn't ask permission, just sinks to his knees beside Bran's chair and wraps an arm around his shoulders. "When you're ready."

"She was six weeks old the day I gave them permission to switch off the machines. And while the ventilator breathed her last breath, her mother was at the house washing down a bottle of sleeping pills with two bottles of vodka. But not before writing a note that would shatter what was left of me."

It's just as hard hearing it the second time, and I don't even try to hold in my tears. I hurt. For him. For Laura. For my brothers and parents.

"The note, which I have locked in a safe deposit box along with Laura's birth and death certificates, told me I wasn't Laura's father. That I'd never slept with Celeste. She lied. And then she named the father. Or fathers. She didn't know exactly who it was, but she was certain of the options."

"How many options? And I stand by my bitch comment,"

Mom mutters, her voice the one she used whenever someone threatened one of us kids when we were little.

"Two."

"Do they know?" Mom's gaze is locked with mine. She's always had this sixth sense when it comes to her kids, and I can see Bran's words have tickled it.

"No. They don't. And I'm not sure they should. It's what I want your advice on. Whether to tell them when there's nothing they can do now. No way for me to make up for being there instead of them."

"It sounds to me like if you hadn't been there, Laura wouldn't exist at all." Dad has moved to the seat beside Bran but his hand remains on Bran's shoulder.

"Probably not. But I have guilt over that. If I hadn't pushed Celeste to have the baby, Laura wouldn't have had such a short life, or been hurt in the most horrible way."

"What if's are a slippery slope and nothing good waits at the bottom." Dad lets go of Bran and leans forward. Pressing his elbows to his knees, he drops his head. "Corbin and Landon."

"What—" Bran's hand jerks in mine.

"It has to be them. It makes sense. Why you'd pull away more after Laura died."

"How did you—"

"Call it a parent's sixth sense. And you can bet my lovely wife came to the same conclusion. Probably before I did."

"They should know. I'll check the game schedule. See when they next have a break. I'd rather tell them here, away from the public eye but we'll all go to New York if we have to. I'm sure we can come up with any number of excuses for us all turning up there." Mom stands and stacks the remaining plates, her movements stilted. "I'll put the dishes on and get dessert.

Nobody needs to help. In fact I'd rather do it on my own, if you don't mind."

We stay silent as she clears the table and heads inside. Once she's out of sight, Dad lets out a harsh breath.

"She's going to have a quiet cry. It's what she does. I think it centers her so she can deal with whatever has her emotional." Dad's gaze meets mine. "She cried the first time you made the Olympic team. Every time after and that includes when you were appointed coach."

Tears are still falling down my face and I have to smile. I don't need to find somewhere quiet to let my emotions out. Not when it comes to this.

BRANTON

It's been two days since I purged my soul in Andrew Watts' arms, then told two people I love deeply they had a grandchild they never knew about. Never met. Have no chance of meeting.

And I hurt more today than I did that night when I crawled into bed.

This is a different hurt though. This is from working my body until I'm on the verge of collapse then pushing it some more. I'm in pain inside and out and there's a thin layer of satisfaction in it.

A new level of penance for all the mistakes I've made.

And a way to avoid thinking about what's to come.

The twins arrive tonight.

Oakley arranged for her grandfather's private jet to fly them here so no one outside the family knows they're coming. After the Knights' game against the Miami Steam, Corbin and Landon will head to the airport, board the plane, and arrive here somewhere around midnight.

Andrew suggested we see what shape they're in before we

151

sit them down and reveal what Celeste's last words were. I'd be happy to wait until morning, but they only have one day before they need to head back to New York.

Part of me wants to get it over with the second they walk through the front door. The other part wants to get in the SUV Blake and I arrived in and drive away. Speed back to my hidey-hole as Blake calls it, and ignore everything and everyone.

I destroyed my friendship with Landon and Corbin when I married Celeste and cut Blake from my life. They saw it as a betrayal, and I know they'll see this as another one. And maybe it is. I've kept this from them—from everyone—for almost three years.

But if I want to get my life back, pursue a relationship with Blake other than being a player on her team, I need to face them with the truth. Have to convince them what I did wasn't with the intent to hurt anyone.

Convince them that I would have told them if I'd known Laura was theirs before the cruelty of her mother took her away.

Pain pinches my chest, and it has nothing to do with the hundred crunches I just completed.

It physically hurts to think of my sweet baby girl gone and I have to lie flat on my back to catch my breath—the pain of her loss takes the wind right out of me.

She might not have been mine biologically but I was there for her first breath. There for her last. And all the ones in between.

She *was* mine.

Sharing her with Blake, with Andrew and Larissa, and soon with Corbin and Landon is harder than I ever thought it would be and she's not here for me to physically hand over. I've been hoarding her memory but what Blake said the other day is true. And subconsciously I think I've known that for a while. It's why I chose to tell Blake outside.

Laura deserves to be in the light, deserves to be shared with people who will love her in spite of her being gone. Keeping her in the dark, in my head and my heart, isn't fair to her or anyone else.

"Are you done killing yourself today?" Blake's voice snaps my head around to find her leaning on the wall near the weights rack.

"Shit. Didn't hear you come in." Reaching for the towel on the mat beside me, I wipe the sweat from my face but I don't get up. I haven't the energy or desire to.

"I've been here since before the lunges."

I cringe. "So a while then."

"Yes." She pushes off the wall and moves closer, sits on the mat next to the one I'm stretched out on. "The physical pain won't take away your emotional pain."

"I know. But it gives me a focus other the tragedy that is my life."

"Having a child, no matter the circumstances, is never a tragedy."

"No, but losing her is." Tightening my stomach, I sit up and drag the towel down my face again. "For more than just me."

"If Celeste had lived, do you think she would have told you? About not being Laura's father?"

"Probably. To hurt me in some way. I have no doubt she would have continued to come around for money even if the divorce had gone through."

"She sounds like a very unhappy woman."

"Having Laura made her that way."

"No. I think she was unhappy long before she got pregnant."

"We'll never know, and to be honest, I hate thinking about her, never mind talking about her. Change of subject. What did you tell Oakley to get the jet?"

"Nothing. Just asked to use it. Pa lets her use it whenever and he's offered it to me before so…" She shrugs.

"Is the plan still to stay here through the rest of the week or are we going to head out on the jet with Corbin and Landon?"

"We're staying. All I've seen so far is a man determined to exhaust himself." Slapping my back before using my shoulder to push to her feet she adds, "Get a shower. Meet us in the kitchen. Mom has the ingredients for your mom's stew. You're cooking tonight."

Tipping my head back, I look up at her. "I thought we were having lasagna."

"Nope. If you need things to keep busy, keep you out of your head, I'll find them for you. I don't want you burning out before I've even gotten you on the ice."

"Ah, so it has nothing to do with you wanting to take care of me."

"It has everything to do with that but right now I'm your coach and I say enough. Hot shower using the massage jets. Then get your chef's hat on."

"Yes, boss." I push up on legs that feel overworked. I knew I was pushing it but I may have pushed more than I thought. I'll be feeling it later. "Where's your dad?"

"In his office. Why?"

"Your mom in the kitchen?"

"No. I think she's out in the garden. Something about enjoying the spring afternoon sun while it lasts. She's predicting snow later in the week."

"I didn't tell them I had Laura's birth certificate changed to add Watts. I want to do that before Landon and Corbin get here."

"Now?"

"I guess. It's been playing on my mind the last few days."

"Tell them at dinner."

"I'd like to do it now."

"Before the shower I told you to take?" Stepping closer, she reaches for my hand and effortlessly weaves our fingers together. "What's going on?"

"I…" Looking away I try to get my thoughts in order. "I need them to know I did the right thing."

"Oh, Bran. You did the right thing the second you made up your mind to get married and have Laura."

"I'm not sure about that, but in the end, after I knew the truth, I did the right thing."

"Do we know the truth? Celeste lied about a lot of things. She could have lied about the twins. They were your closest friends, she had to know that. If she was going to name anyone to hurt you, they were the perfect choice."

"I have Laura's DNA."

"What? Why?"

"I asked them to run hers and mine because I'd started to wonder, especially after she tried to hook up with Carl again."

"And the results? When did you get those?"

"The day I turned up to the Knights game smashed out of my head."

"Bran." Her arms are around me so fast I don't have time to react. I'm drenched in sweat and stink worse than a skunk but Blake doesn't care. She wraps me up and holds me tight.

At first I don't move. I'm incapable of doing anything except soak up her warmth, but the longer she holds on to me, the harder it is to stop myself from returning the embrace.

And my dick isn't oblivious to the situation.

We've managed to keep things between us platonic for the most part. I've had more than one hard on since Blake arrived back in my life but this is the first time I've had one with her plastered against me.

I'm not going to lie, I'd give anything to move us out of the friends zone except I can't afford to fuck this up and pushing her to the floor and fucking her now would definitely be fucking this up.

"I want—"

"I know, Bran. I do too but we can't, it's not our time."

How she reads me, the situation, with ease makes my affection for her grow. I'm in love with her. Have always been in love with her. I just never had the balls to go after what we could have.

Hindsight is a wonderful thing for making you look like a fool. And I was the biggest fool of them all.

I had Blake Watts.

Could have had her since I was twenty and I chose ambition—mine and hers—the NHL, her Olympic success, over making our connection solid.

And for what?

Another woman to come along and blow up all the plans we'd talked about.

"You will never understand how sorry I am about what happened," I whisper into her hair.

"Stop beating yourself up over things we can't change." She leans back and locks eyes with me. "And I say 'we' because we both did things, let things happen, that we should have pushed through together on. We could have made it work long distance. I know we could have, and yet neither of us pushed for that when we should have."

"No more. From now on we tackle everything together. I don't think I can do it without you anyway."

"Good thing you don't have to."

"I'd give anything to kiss you right now but if I do I don't think I can stop at a kiss."

"We'll save it for later. After the twins have gone back to New York."

Loosening my hold, I move back and she lets her arms slip away from me. "If we're waiting…" I glance down at my tented shorts.

Blake's laughter lights up the room, lights up my insides.

"It's not that funny."

"I'm not laughing because it's funny. I'm laughing because I'm happy. Seeing you, being with you, makes me happier than I've been in years. And I wasn't even unhappy."

With a last smile she leaves me to think about what just transpired and to get my dick under control. I'm not about to walk through her parents' house with a blatant erection. And the hand towel I have in my fist isn't going to give much coverage and would look more obvious than my crotch tent.

Shaking my head I think about the things we have to navigate before I can kiss Blake the way I want to.

The thought of her brothers is the ice bath my libido needs for instant deflation.

BLAKE

The noise my brothers make coming through the front door is enough to wake the whole house.

Good thing no one is sleeping. We're in the living room, where we settled after dinner.

Bran didn't hunt down Mom and Dad before we ate like he wanted. Instead he waited to tell them over dessert what he did for Laura, for the twins, for them.

I could have predicted my parents' response to his words. Could easily have told Bran he'd have my mom in tears before she could leave the room and my dad close.

Since then we left the subject alone, all of us aware we'd be revisiting it once Corbin and Landon arrived. Instead we've talked about the Rogues and how Bran wants to sign the contract we offered without an agent's input but I won't let him.

Dad in his typical fashion decided he and Bran would call Drake tomorrow afternoon and iron out the deal between Bran and his new agent before setting said agent loose on the deal with the Rogues.

I love that my dad is taking an active role in Bran reclaiming his life. I know he had a lot of input into Bran's previous deal, the same as he's done with my brothers over the years. And I know I don't have to worry about Bran on that end. Not when he has my dad at his back.

No, what I have to worry about are the two men standing in the living room doorway with angry scowls on their faces.

"What the fuck is he doing here?" Landon demands, his voice loud and harsh as he steps into the quiet room.

"There will be none of that in my house. From either of you." Mom gives both my brothers a look that used to have us shaking in our shoes when we were little. It has the same effect now.

"Sorry, Mom," Landon says at a more acceptable volume, his angry eyes dropping from Bran for a moment.

"So you should be. Now come over here and give me a hug." She stands from the couch but doesn't move toward them. She's showing them where her support lies. And right now, after Bran revealed he gave Laura her name as a homage to her and his mom as well as the last name Watts, she's firmly in his corner.

Corbin sends me a look. He's always been the more circumspect of the two of them, Landon the hot head who lets his mouth—and actions—run away from him more often than not. But Corbin's look. It has me thinking and before anyone can say anything else I'm on my feet.

"You know!"

Corbin glances at Landon before meeting my gaze head on. "I know a lot of things."

"Don't. Don't you dare give me the runaround on this."

Bran's hand presses into my lower back when he stands beside me. "What? What are you talking about?"

"Corbin knows. He knows what you're going to tell him."

"What? How?"

My brother looks at everyone in the room and I know he's trying to gauge our emotions, the possibility of his words causing the already volatile situation to explode. With a deep sigh, he locks eyes with Landon.

"Celeste came to me after she married Bran. Told me the baby wasn't Bran's."

Bran goes rigid beside me. "Why didn't you tell me she did that?"

"Because she was full of shit. She told Landon I fucked her—sorry for the language Mom—when I didn't."

"Then..."

"No. Your daughter wasn't mine. I never touched the woman. I wouldn't touch her if she were the last woman on the planet," Corbin growls.

Everyone turns to Landon. It's only a second late that he grips his head.

"Fuck!"

The curse is loud, ragged, filled with agony and no one moves, pretty sure there isn't even a drawn-in breath.

"That fucking bitch!"

In the blink of an eye, Landon is gone. Corbin turns to follow but Dad jumps up and grips his shoulder, holds him in place.

"No. Let him go. Explain what happened and why your brother seems oblivious to it."

"He's oblivious because I didn't want her getting her claws in him again. She did a good job of snowing him and screwing with his head the first time and it wasn't until she lied about me sleeping with her that he saw her true colors."

"He would never believe you'd do that," I say. "Because you would *never* do that."

"No, I wouldn't." Corbin turns his gaze to Bran. "I swear,

if I believed her, I would have said something in spite of you cutting us out. I would have made you listen."

"I..." Bran swallows hard. "I honestly don't know that I would have. I was in protection mode."

"You would need an armored suit to protect yourself from her."

"Son." Mom moves to Corbin, cradles his jaw with her hand. "Tell me why Landon had the reaction he did."

"I'm not sure. He hasn't said anything, but I know when Bran and Celeste got married, he went crazy for a bit. He didn't tell me details but I know he saw her the week before we found out."

"You think she told him about the baby?" Dad asks.

Shaking his head, Corbin says, "No. There's no way he knew before the rest of the world. He would never have let Bran marry her if he thought there was a chance she was pregnant with his baby."

"The woman seems to have been filled with lies."

"And venom," Corbin adds to Mom's assessment. "Lies and venom and she'd turn it on anyone in her way."

"But I don't understand why she would lie to me about the night of the party. Why tell me we slept together and then come at me weeks later? What was her goal?"

"She wanted Landon. He ditched her when she tried to drive a wedge between us. She did it the whole time they were together and for a while it was only little things, things he could overlook but the lie about me and her? Yeah, that was too big a deal to ignore. They had a huge argument because he also found out she'd hooked up with Carl Burgan a few times when they were first together. That was the end for Landon."

"So why did he see her the week before she came to me?" Bran asks.

"I honestly don't know. All he told me was that they'd

spoken, that she told him to fuck off and he'd be sorry for letting her go."

"Was he sorry?" Mom asks. "Because I'm not sure what was going through his head just now other than distress."

"No. He's been seeing someone. A woman he met at a cafe."

"He's got a girlfriend?"

"I wouldn't call her that exactly, but they hang out. A lot. He hasn't been with anyone since the debacle with Celeste. As I said, she did a number on his head." Corbin glances over his shoulder. "I'm not sure how this is going to affect him."

"So you know what I'm going to say?" Bran asks.

"I'm assuming you're here to tell us Celeste said Landon is Laura's father. What I don't understand is why you're only now telling anyone."

"I didn't know until after Laura... After Celeste..."

"How is that possible?"

"She left a note. Wrote it while washing down a bottle of sleeping pills with two bottles of vodka."

"Jesus." Corbin's gaze moves to Dad. "Someone needs to go find him."

"I think it should be Branton." Mom's words have us all looking at her. "I think it's between the two of them at this point."

"But—"

"No." Mom cuts Corbin off. "She played the two of them. Pitted them against each other even if they weren't aware of it. I think they both have insight into her that the other can use to understand more of the situation and possibly move past the damage she caused each of them."

"And they have that in common to bring them back together," Dad adds with a nod.

"And me?" Corbin's gaze flits between Mom and Dad. "How do I fit into this?"

"You don't yet." Bran leaves my side and goes to my brother. "After, once Landon and I have cleared the air. Then we'll both need you to add what you know."

"I don't know much more than what I just told you all."

"No. Maybe not. But you know Landon, you were there when he was seeing Celeste, which I was clueless about, by the way. How the hell were they together and I not know?"

Corbin shrugs. "I didn't know he'd been seeing her until he was three months in. I told you, she tried to drive a wedge between us, most of that was done by her insisting they keep their relationship a secret."

"I don't understand this woman at all," Mom mumbles.

"I was married to her, lived in the same house as her, for months, and *I* don't understand her." Bran rubs a hand over his chin. "I'm beginning to think I'll never understand."

"That might be, but do you need to now? She's no longer in your life, and you're doing your best to move past what happened, to reclaim the man you used to be—"

"I'll never reclaim him." Bran cuts me off. "He no longer exists. She made sure of that because I'll never have the ability to trust anyone at their word again. She stripped that away. That naive belief in people being honest."

"But she hasn't done that. All she's done is make you more cautious. You still trust people, Bran. You trust *me*."

"I have always, will always, trust you. You've never once lied to me. Never once done anything to hurt me or manipulate me. If anything, you've always let me control our relationship and I'm sorry I put you through that. I will never do that again."

"Bran."

"No. I know you could have fought against me, you should

have, but you didn't. And after this is over, after I set things straight with Landon, I'm going to show you my appreciation of that. Of you. Every day for the rest of my life. If you'll let me."

I have no words. We've talked about how we feel, what we want, but he's basically just declared his intentions in front of my parents, my brother.

It doesn't matter how things turn out with Landon, I will do everything—anything—to make sure we get the chance we should have had, the chance Celeste derailed when she set out to hurt two of the most important men my life.

The chance Bran—*I*—deserve.

BRANTON

It doesn't take me long to find Landon.

He's in the basement smacking the shit out of puck after puck in the small rink Andrew built for us all to practice our shooting.

I let him finish the bucket of pucks before I interrupt. His form is good. If anything, it's a little sharper than it was a couple of years ago. The last time we played together.

"You want to get in goal and let me fire some of these at you?"

Landon's words bring a small smile to my mouth. "No. I suck at goaltending. You know that."

The grunt he gives is neither agreement or argument and he continues to fire the pucks into the net.

When the final slap is complete, the puck buried in the back of the net, Landon lowers his head and doesn't move.

I don't know if I should get closer, say something, or let him work it out. He's always been the one to initiate. His hot-headedness, his lack of filter, always meant he was the first to speak, the first to react to any situation.

The fact he seems to be struggling to do anything right now worries me more than any of the arguments we had when I married Celeste. "Why didn't you tell me you were seeing her?"

With a deep sigh, he reaches for the bucket and lifts it. Glancing over his shoulder, I see the ravaged expression on his face and for the first time in a long time I wish I could reach out and draw him into a hug.

We used to be close, the three of us; from the age of six up, we were inseparable. That changed during college, but when we all ended up contracted to the Knights, we rebuilt our friendship back to what it had always been.

Until Celeste turned up on my doorstep.

Then again, maybe the change had come when she'd gotten her claws into Landon.

"I didn't tell anyone."

His words have my gaze snapping up to his face. I'd been watching him scoop the pucks together ready to put them back in the bucket and hadn't noticed he'd turned to look at me. "Not even Corbin? Why?"

"She didn't want anyone to know. Said it would make it harder for us to be together because the media would be all over it. Because of her history."

"And you believed that? Accepted that excuse to hide behind closed doors?" I'd never know Landon to be secretive which makes this whole situation more fucked up. That she had that kind of control over him.

He shrugs. "Wasn't my finest moment."

"I get that, but I thought..."

"I know." His gaze drops to the ice before bouncing back up. "I let us all down, most of all you. I had no idea she was going to do what she did. I should have. The morning I caught her coming out of your room—"

"What?" His words have me taking a step back. "You saw?"

He gives a quick nod. "She was still doing up her shirt and I could see through the gap in the doorway that you hadn't bother to get dressed yet. You weren't even out of bed."

"I didn't see you. I told her to get out. Pretty sure I yelled it."

"I didn't hear if you did, but the smug look she gave me as we passed"—he shakes his head—"I knew it was my fault, knew she'd hooked up with you to get at me and I should have warned you but by then I'd had enough of her. I just wanted her out of my life. Figured you'd be shot of her soon enough. We all knew you were waiting for Blake."

"We were waiting for each other."

"I never understood that."

I shake my head, a rueful smile curling my lips. "I'm beginning to think I don't anymore either."

"You planning to fix that now?"

"We're working on it."

"Are you going to sign on with the Rogues?"

"Yeah."

We're quiet for a few moments. Both caught up in our own thoughts. Then Landon lets a deep sigh loose, his shoulders lower, and his gaze meets mine.

"The week before you got married, I bumped into her. Celeste. She gloated about the great guy she was seeing and how I'd regret letting her go. I told her the only regret I had was meeting her in the first place and I was glad she was out of my life. Wanna know what she said to that?"

"I'm sure it was a blade to the gut."

"Might as well have been."

"What did she say?"

"She said I could go fuck myself and I wouldn't be rid of her like I thought because her and the guy she was seeing were planning to get married. Have a family." He looks off to the side. "You know one of the only arguments we had other than about Corbin was the fact she didn't want a family. Ever. Which now, looking back, seems like a stupid discussion to be having with a woman I'd been with for only a handful of months."

"She told you she was going to do what you wanted but not with you?"

"Yeah. Then she married you."

"Only because she was pregnant and asked for money to fix the problem."

"Fuck!" Landon pulls back his stick and sends a puck at the wall. It's quickly followed by several more before he launches the stick after them. "She was mine, wasn't she? That's why you're here, why Dad called us home and sent Oakley fucking James's jet to get us."

"Yes. But I didn't know. Not until after Celeste killed herself. After she—"

"I hate to speak ill of the dead but good fucking riddance."

"I agree."

"What the fuck do we do now, Bran? Where the fuck do we go from here? I missed—" he chokes on his final words.

"I'd like to share her with you. Laura. I have pictures. Videos."

Landon is nodding but his face says he doesn't want to see anything.

"We can wait. I have everything in storage. Some other things in a safe deposit box."

"I..." He skates over to his stick and picks it up. Checks it for damage. "I need time to process everything."

"I can understand that. I've spent a couple of years processing. It wasn't until Blake showed up. Until Oakley dumped a bucket of water on my head."

A short bark of laughter escapes Landon before he mutters, "A story for another day."

"Yes."

"We're good. We will be. I just…"

"Need time."

"Yeah." He looks at me, sorrow and apology in his gaze and I want to tell him he has nothing to be sorry for, that I'm sorry. "I don't know if I'll be ready before I leave tomorrow night."

"I'm okay with that. But if you could unblock my number, that would be good."

My words get a smile, which was the aim, and I hope he doesn't take as long as I did to process. I hope he has questions I can answer. I hope he wants me to share Laura with him. He deserves to know her even if she hadn't really begun to show her personality yet. Even if the smiles I swore she gave me were only wind.

"This is totally fucked up."

"Not going to argue that." I can't. Everything about my interactions with Celeste were fucked up. Everything except Laura.

"Can you tell them I'm okay? I don't want them coming down here. If you can run interference for the rest of tonight."

"I can do that. But I need to tell you one more thing before I leave you to process."

"Yeah, what?"

"After I read Celeste's note, the one fueled by alcohol and sleeping pills, I had Laura's birth certificate changed."

"To what?"

I can see the hope in his eyes, the yearning for something he'll never really have, and I need him to understand why I did it the way I did. "I changed her name. Left mine as the father but changed hers to Laura Jean Lattimer Watts."

I watch as Landon's eyes fill with tears and I know he can see mine have done the same.

"There were legal reasons to keep me listed as her father, but I don't think I could have given you that anyway, but she needed to have part of you. She *was* part of you."

"The best part."

I offer him a smile. "Yeah, the best part."

"I will want to know. To see. Just not yet. I…"

"I get it. When you're ready, I'll be waiting."

"In Baton Rouge?"

I can't stop the grin spreading across my face. "Yeah. In Baton Rouge. With your sister." I have to add the last part. Need him to know, like I did the rest of her family upstairs, that I'm serious about being with Blake. She's my future and I'm not talking about her being my coach.

"You deserve to find happiness. Both of you. After you got married… Blake, she…"

"We've talked about it. Will talk about it more I'm sure. But neither of us is putting our careers ahead of our relationship ever again. I'd never play again if it means being without Blake."

"She'd never make you choose."

"She never did before."

"No. She wouldn't."

"She stood back and let me take the lead. Look where that got us. From now on she calls the shots. Both on and off the ice and I'll be the happiest man in the world if she'll do it for the rest of my life."

"You love her."

"I've *always* loved her. *Will* always love her. Never thought I stood a chance until she was there for me after Mom died. Pulled me out of that darkness and showed me the light. And she's doing that all over again now."

"She loves you too."

"I hope so. But even if she only feels a fraction of what I do, I'll be the luckiest guy on earth."

"You should probably buy yourself a lottery ticket."

"No need. If Blake loves me, I've already hit the jackpot."

BLAKE

After Bran leaves to find Landon, the rest of us talk a little more before calling it a night. Mom and Dad headed off to their side of the house holding hands, whispering in each other's ears. Corbin gives me a tight hug and a sad smile, before heading to the room he and Landon shared when they lived at home and continue to use whenever they're here.

And I do something I've never done before.

I take the back hallway to the suite of rooms Bran and his mother lived in from the day they arrived in Westwood.

It's bizarre to think I've never actually set foot in this part of the house. Not when I was younger, before Bran and his mom arrived, not when I was a teenager still living under my parents' roof, and not in all the years since.

This has been my family's home my entire life. Up until I bought my place in Baton Rouge two years ago, this house was my home. And not once did I think about coming to this part of it.

The walls are the same color as the rest of the house, the

furnishings a little more worn—faded—and I imagine they were Loretta's choices, unchanged from when she was alive.

They feel like her. Which is a strange thing to say but it doesn't make the feeling any less real.

I feel like she could step into the room at any moment. Like she hasn't been gone for six years.

I wonder how Bran felt sleeping here again after all that time.

Once he went away to college, he never returned for more than a day or two. Not until his mother was killed and even then, I don't remember him staying down here. Mom put him upstairs in one of the guest rooms. To be closer to the twins—to family. She didn't want him here alone with his grief and memories.

Although now I'm thinking about it, I'm pretty sure no one slept the night before or the night of Loretta's funeral. Her death—the suddenness of it—had been a huge shock to all of us, left a gaping hole we all struggled with.

Not once in the last few days has he mentioned anything about staying here, or his mom, so I have to assume he's comfortable. And glancing around I see signs of his comfort, signs he's been here. A shirt draped over a chair, shoes kicked off beside the couch, an empty glass on the counter of the small kitchenette.

I can see and feel his presence, and that offers me a small amount of relief. To know he's made himself at home when in reality this is no longer his home and hasn't been for a while—if he ever thought of it as home.

I don't want to intrude but I also don't want to be hovering like a weirdo in his living room when he's finished with Landon and finds his way back here.

And I'm honest enough to admit I want to see where he's been sleeping, where he slept all those years ago when he was a teenager and nothing more to me than my brothers' friend, our housekeeper's son, another competitor on the ice.

Leaving a lamp on in the living room, I switch off all the other lights as I make my way toward the bedrooms. It's a short hall, a door on either side and one at the end. All open.

In front of me is the bathroom. To the left must have been his mom's room with its frilly lace bedding, and to the right, with its unmade twin bed, has to be Bran's room.

Stopping in the doorway, I can't bring myself to step inside; it feels like an invasion of privacy and yet...

My gaze is drawn to the desk in the far corner.

The surface is bare except for Bran's wallet and a single photo frame. Off to one side, it's not the silver frame that holds my gaze, it's the picture in it. A picture that pulls me over the threshold with a visceral tug.

It's me and Bran.

I don't remember when it was taken—I've never seen it before, but I recognize the couch we're sitting on. It's the one my brothers still have. The one they refuse to get rid of even though they bought a huge monstrosity for their living room and it's now relegated to an unused bedroom in their apartment.

My mind spins. With memories and confusion. I bought them the couch. As a house-warming present the year they signed with the Knights and moved in to an apartment together with Bran in New York.

"I won't let them get rid of it."

Bran's voice startles me but I'm too stuck on the picture to turn. We look so happy. "Why?"

"Because you bought it for us."

"I didn't. I bought it for them. I bought you..." I'd bought him a bed. He'd only had the twin he'd used the entire time he'd been in college and refused to buy anything bigger even though he had the money.

"A king bed." He's closer now, right behind me if the heat I feel at my back is any indication. "I still have it. In storage along with the rest of my stuff. I never took any of it to the house. Bought everything new for that."

"They still have the couch. It's in your old bedroom. Where your bed used to be."

"I know. I asked them to keep it there for the occasional night I still crashed at their place after I moved out."

"I don't understand why you would ask that or why they would agree to it."

"Some things aren't explainable."

"When was this photo taken?"

"The summer before I got my own place. The apartment I'd hoped to share with you."

I'd known. The minute he told me he'd found a place, signed a lease, I'd known he would ask me to move in with him. But I'd gotten a call from Hockey Canada, about working with the national women's team, coaching them for the Olympics, and he hadn't asked...

And I hadn't offered.

Within months he'd married a woman I'd never met, knew nothing about except what was splashed across the internet, and was expecting a baby.

"We never really talked about what we wanted." The words are out of my mouth before I think them and I know it's something we need to address. Why hadn't we *talked*?

"We made vague statements about the future. About what we'd do, but you're right, we never really talked about it being *us* together in that future. I'm sorry we didn't. Sorry we both assumed we were on the same page. So sorry."

"But we were on the same page. Weren't we?"

"Yes."

"I don't want to do it again. I know there aren't any guarantees in life and things can change in a heartbeat, but I don't want to leave either of us in the dark, assuming but not really knowing. No more vague future plans, no more this is what I'd like or want." I spin on my heel and face him. He's close, like I thought. So close that when I tip my chin up to meet his gaze, our lips are a breath apart. "If we do this—"

"We *are* doing this."

"Then we need to be clear."

"How's this for clear? I *will* play for the Rogues. I *will* move in with you. I *will* live with you. I *will* sleep in your bed. I *will* put a ring on your finger when you're ready. I *will* build a life with you. A life filled with love and family and anything else we want."

His declaration, because that's what it is, bring tears to my eyes, makes my nose sting and my throat tight, but I push out my own intentions. "I *will* coach the Rogues. I *will* move in with you. I *will* live with you. I *will* sleep in your bed. I *will* put a ring on your finger when I'm ready. I *will* build a life with you. A life filled with love and family and children and every damn wish either of us ever has."

"I have a lot of wishes, Blake."

"I want to give you every last one of them."

"You already have."

"When do we start?"

"Now. We start now."

His mouth claims mine for the first time in our lives and I'm drowning in so many sensations. Love and want and need and regret.

Why haven't we ever done this?

He tastes like the wine from dinner, a touch of the chocolate and berry tart from dessert. Sweet and spicy with a touch of decadence and I can't get enough.

I never want to stop, want to keep kissing him until neither of us can breathe or remember our names.

I'm not sure who moves first. Who grabs and pulls—pushes.

One minute we're standing, the next we're on the floor.

Urgency rushes through my veins and my fingers grip harder, my nails digging in to tear at fabric in my way. I want the barriers between us gone. Every last one of them.

We've broken down the emotional ones, all that's left is to sort through the rubble and rebuild; now I want to rip away the physical ones. I want nothing and no one to stop us from coming together.

"Blake." Bran growls my name into my mouth, his lips sliding over mine as he speaks. "I never fucked her."

His words stop me. My eyes find his but I can't decipher what he's saying.

"I never had sex with Celeste. You know that. And this probably isn't the time, but I need you to understand what you mean to me. Need you to know I've never done this with anyone else. Never wanted anyone but you. It's why I was so confused about what happened, about the lies she told."

"Wait. Wait. Wait. What are you saying?"

He swallows, his eyes searching mine, love and desire and concern rolling through their navy-blue depths.

"I've never had sex."

BRANTON

Way to ruin the moment, kill the mood, dickhead.

If I wouldn't look like more of an idiot, I'd slap myself upside the head.

"You... *Never?*" Blake's eyes are locked on mine, confusion swirling in their silver depths. "But... Why?"

I can't lie to her. *Won't* lie to her. "It's aways been you."

"Branton, you're twenty-six years old, have been married, have had puck bunnies throwing themselves at you since high school and you're telling me you've never had sex with anyone?"

"No. I never wanted anyone but you. Thought my dick might be broken somehow but it all works just fine." I rock my hips against hers to show her how well things are working.

"You've done nothing? Because I've got to say, you kiss like an expert."

"Ah, well, I've kissed a couple of girls—women. Not many but a few." I know my cheeks are red. I'm waving the virgin flag high over my head right now. "It never went far. My mind

178

wanted to, thought I should, you know, but my body—my heart—had other ideas."

"I don't know what to say. This is...unbelievable. Extraordinary."

"Is that a good extraordinary or bad?" If my lack of experience turns her off... "I might not have firsthand knowledge but I'm not clueless. I'll make it good for you."

"I don't think you're clueless or can't make me feel good, I just... I'm shocked." She wiggles under me. "And my ass is going numb."

"Shit." Jackknifing up, I jump to my feet and reach down to pull her up beside me. "Sorry. We kind of rushed that and I... Shit. I've killed the mood, haven't I?"

"No. No. You did neither of those things. As I said, I'm shocked by your revelation. And in awe that you waited. For me."

"I didn't tell you to change anything between us, I just want you to know what you mean to me. What you've always meant to me."

"I'm honored. And I have to admit a little thrilled I'm the only one who will ever share this with you. I'm excited to explore this together because I might not be as pure as you but I'm not far off it. I've only sleep with three guys. It's hard to trust anyone to let them that close. I haven't been with anyone since your second year of college. The year we got close when..."

"When Mom was killed."

"Yeah. I wasn't seeing anyone for a while before that and after... Well, after, I felt like I belonged to you. Or maybe it was I didn't feel like I belonged with anyone else." She shrugs. "It's hard to explain."

"I get it. Believe me, I get it. Being a hormone riddled teenager who can't get it up for anyone but his best friends' older sister is extremely hard to explain. Not that I tried. Can you imagine the teasing I would have gotten?"

Her mouth splits into a grin, her lips quickly parting on a laugh.

"Yeah, you can laugh."

"My brothers would have had a field day with that info."

I shudder at the thought.

She has to suck in a breath as another burst of laughter breaks free. "Oh, god. They really would have been merciless."

"I've kept this secret for years, I'm trusting you to keep it with me." I'm not. I don't care if she tells anyone. Nothing matters to me any more except having Blake, claiming her as my own. The world knowing she's mine.

"I would never talk to them about my sex life, why the hell would I talk to them about yours?"

It's my turn to shrug. "Don't know. Not sure why I said that."

"Okay, here's the deal. From now on, from this minute, my secrets are your secrets, and your secrets are my secrets."

"Deal. Should we shake on it or..."

"Oh. I think we can seal this deal with something better than a handshake." Her hands find my waist, her fingers curling into the waistband of my pants. "But first we'll need to get rid of these clothes."

"Can I admit to a teenage fantasy and maybe convince you to make it a reality?"

"Of course, I told you I want to make all your wishes come true."

I can't believe I'm going to tell her about this, ask her to turn it real. "I used to lie on that bed and think about you upstairs, in the shower. I'd imagine you coming down here in only a towel because the lights have gone out and nobody else is home. You'd ask to sleep with me because you're scared of the storm raging outside..."

"This is sounding very elaborate."

"I had a vivid imagination when it came to you. Still do."

"Oh?"

"Yeah. Now I'm thinking maybe I pulled you in here out of that storm and you're soaked to the skin, freezing cold, and I need to do everything I can to warm you up."

"Like?"

"Body heat. Body heat is the best and fastest way to raise your temperature."

"Pretty sure my temp is already rising."

"Let's see how high we can get it."

I don't waste time ridding us of our clothes. I've seen Blake in a swimsuit, in gym gear, but never completely naked. Never with only light covering her body.

She's built—from all the years of hockey—strong and powerful, and I'm relieved I won't need to temper my own strength. Because now that I have her, now that she's naked in my arms, I'm not sure I can hold back.

I've waited years to touch her, to taste her, to be hers. And that's what it comes down to. I'm offering her me. A virgin for her to deflower.

"What's with that smirk?"

My gaze meets hers, my smile growing wider. "I'm the virgin sacrifice."

Laughing, she rolls her eyes. "Are we changing your fantasy again?"

"You are my fantasy. Any way I can have you."

"You have me, Bran, any way you want."

"I just want you. I need you. More than I've ever needed anything and for a while there I lost my way, lost you, and I'll never forgive myself for that."

"We'll make up for it."

"You bet we will."

"Tell me what you want, what you need, what to do."

"Lie with me." Reaching over, I pull back the bed covers. "I want to sleep in this bed with you."

"Only sleep?"

"No. But I'll take anything I can get. Sleeping beside you is just as much a fantasy as fucking you."

"Such a crude mouth for an innocent virgin." Blake smirks at me before she climbs on the bed.

"I told you I'm not clueless." Slipping under the covers after her, I wrap an arm around her waist and pull her against me, chest to chest.

My eyes close as a shiver of pleasure rolls through me.

Her soft skin pressed to mine is a touch I've waited a lifetime for and I'm going to savor it. Every second, every inch. I want to etch tonight on my memory like a blade scores the ice. Except unlike an ice rink there will be no mental resurfacer to clear the marks away.

I will never forget our first time.

"You smell good." The tip of her nose brushes against my neck, sending a shiver down my spine. "So good I'm not sure if I want to lick or bite you."

"How about kissing me?" Using a finger under her chin, I tilt her head back so I can see her face, her eyes. "Will you kiss me again?"

"Of course. You don't have to ask."

"So I can kiss you whenever I want?"

"Always."

"Now?"

"Yes."

"In front of your family?"

"Yes."

"In front of our team?"

"Ah, well, that might be somewhere we have to refrain…"

"If there's a ring on your finger? On mine?"

"Oh, well, that would be different."

"Then let's get married. Tomorrow."

Blake opens her mouth, but nothing comes out. Her eyes are full of shock and I take advantage of her frozen state to kiss the ever-loving-shit out of both of us.

By the time I'm done, we're breathless, panting hard, and I do the only thing I can think of.

"Marry me, Blake. Make me the happiest man alive by making me your husband. I promise to take care of you, always put you first—"

Her hand slaps over my mouth. "Bran. We've just…we haven't…we…"

"You know it's right." My words are muffled against her palm. My gaze locked with hers. "You know this is where we're going, where we should already be. Haven't we wasted enough time?"

"But…" She slowly lowers her hand and I reach for it, curl our fingers together.

"What's stopping you from saying yes?"

"I…" She shakes her head like she's trying to shake her thoughts loose.

"When I asked, what was the first word to pop into your head? Don't lie."

"Yes."

Grinning, I bring my free hand up and cradle her face. "Then that's the answer. Think about why you couldn't say it."

"Because there's so much going on, so many things outside of us—"

"None of those are important when it comes to this decision. *We* are the most important thing, everything else should be decided around that. We're already moving in together, we've made a verbal commitment to each other about our future. This is the next step. The one we should have taken a long time ago."

"We should have gotten married already?"

"You don't think that's where we'd be by now if I hadn't gotten caught up in some woman's revenge scheme?"

"You think Celeste did what she did for revenge?"

"Yes. After talking to Landon, I think she did everything to get back at him for not doing what she wanted."

"Do you blame Landon for that?"

"Of course not. Why would I?"

"Yes!" Her mouth smashes on mine, her tongue thrusting between my lips, my teeth, and I'm barely able to reciprocate the kiss before she's pulling back.

"Yes. Let's get married."

"Tomorrow?"

"You don't want to wait? Have everyone there? You didn't get to do—"

"As far as I'm concerned, I've never been married before. I had a legal contract—a business arrangement—with a woman to secure a child. Nothing more."

"Okay, however you want to do it, we'll do it."

"Speaking of doing it." I press my mouth to hers and roll her beneath me. My hips slip into the cradle of hers, my thighs pushing her legs wide, and my dick notches in her heated core. I'm not embarrassed to admit I'm close to blowing my load. "This first time will be too fast."

"I don't mind fast."

"I do. I want to love you slowly."

"It doesn't matter how you love me, Bran, as long as you love me."

"I do. Love you. With everything I am I love you, and I can guarantee that will never change."

Blake

I don't remember the last time I had sex. Don't remember the guy. But then none of my previous sexual encounters were memorable. And even if they were, Bran would be wiping my memory clean of anyone or anything before this.

I know my own body, have given myself pleasure whenever the urge struck, but he seems to have a direct line to—insider knowledge of—every erogenous point from my head to my toes.

And he's hitting every one of them.

His lips are soft and brushing, then hard and pressing. His hands, sweeping and slow, then gripping and fast. It's like he can't decide how he wants to touch me—where he wants to touch me—from one second to the next.

The quick shift in sensation, the moans of pleasure rushing over my skin, the sound of my own heartbeat pulsing in my ears, has my insides coiling tighter and tighter. Heat throbs in my pussy, liquid seeps from my core, and I can't stand the wait, don't want it to end.

I'm writhing beneath him, searching for the right pressure,

the right spot, my hands clawing at his shoulders to pull him closer, my legs wrapping around his to hold him against me harder.

"*Bran.*"

"It's okay," he murmurs against my belly, his tongue tickling my skin. "I just need to taste you."

"I can't wait." As much as I want to feel his mouth on me, I want to feel him deep inside more. "I want you now."

He nips my hip. "You have me."

"No. I want—" Air rushes through my teeth, choking off my words, when his tongue swipes up the center of my pussy.

He didn't lie. He's not clueless. He knows what I want, what I need, before I do; before I have a chance to enjoy each touch he's giving me another, a different one, a new sensation that has my belly twisting tighter.

I can't breathe, can't think, can't do more than hold on, and hold on I do. My hands on his head, my fingers tangled in his hair.

And when he adds his fingers to the mix, I'm done. Arching up and crying out, I ride the most intense orgasm of my life.

I'm breathless and boneless, and when his mouth lands on mine, the taste of me on his lips, his cock pressing into my clenching flesh, I open my legs wider, urge him deeper.

I can't articulate my thoughts because Bran's mouth hasn't left mine, but he doesn't need a verbal clue; he's either well aware of my needs or handling his own.

With a brutal shove, he thrusts his cock deep inside me. There's an ache of need, of pain, of pleasure. A second of panic. Then he pulls out, pushes in, pulls out, pushes in, and I'm lost to the frantic rhythm he sets.

A dance as old as time we've never engaged in before but seem to know with a lifetime of knowledge.

It isn't like anything I remember. Like anything I could have imagined.

His tongue mimics his cock, racing in and out of my mouth, taking—giving.

Heat curls in my pussy, a pounding swirl of pleasure that consumes every part of me. A tingling twist, a hollow swoop, and I'm losing myself again.

A surprised cry bursts from me into him and not a second later he tenses, his body rigid on mine, his cock buried deeper than before.

With a grunt he jerks, and drenching heat explodes inside me.

I don't know how we move, when we move, but we're pressed together on our sides, breathing hard and holding tight.

I can't find words.

Don't know why I'm trying.

What just happened says more than any words I can come up with.

"I knew it would be like this."

"Hmm..." I barely manage a sound.

"I think I was scared of this. Scared of giving in and having you. I knew I'd never survive losing this. Losing you."

"Love is the greatest risk of all."

"She used to say that all the time."

"She knew what she was talking about."

"She also used to say only the brave receive the ultimate prize."

"Your mother was a very wise woman."

"She would have loved this for us." He lifts his head to look at me, his eyes shining with love. "She knew. Told me I shouldn't waste my time going after a prize that was fleeting, not when I already had the ultimate prize."

Loretta Lattimer had never spoken to me about Bran's crush when we were kids but I'd known she could see it. Everyone could see it. "I want to name our first daughter after her."

"I... What?"

"We just had unprotected sex, Bran. I'm not on anything. No need."

"So we—" His gaze drops between us. "Wow."

"You said you wanted to get married tomorrow."

"Can we sneak off now, take Mr. James's jet to Vegas and get married tonight?" His eyes are back on mine, excitement making them sparkle. "I don't want to wait. And if we didn't hit the jackpot tonight, we'll keep trying."

"Bran, we've got—"

"I know. A lot going on. A lot to do. I need to get in game shape, you need to build a team. We'll do it together while we build our family."

"We should wait until—"

"No. I don't want to wait for any of it. I learned a lot in the few weeks I had with Laura. I want to be a dad again. I loved it. I'm good at it. And I want to hold a piece of you and me. The best piece of you and me. Our child will be visible proof of our love. I want to show that to the world."

"I'll talk to Mom and Dad in the morning. See if we can go somewhere local tomorrow, and if we can't get married right away, we'll get things sorted so we can do it as soon as we can. I want to get married in Canada. It's the only thing I'll ask for."

"As much as rushing out of here right this second appeals, I want to give you what you want. I don't care as long as I get my ring on your finger. *Oh!*"

Before I can ask what's wrong, Bran has disengaged our bodies, slipped out of bed, and run from the room. His actions should make me panic but I know he's not running away and my belief is confirmed a minute later.

"Here!" He rushes back into the room. Drops to his knees beside the bed and grasps my left hand. "It was the ring my dad gave Mom. She never wore it after we came here. Told me where she kept it so when the time was right, I could give it to the love of my life."

"Oh, Bran, it's beautiful." The cool metal slides up my finger, the solitaire winking and flashing as the overhead light hits it.

"I know it's not big, the diamond, but it would mean the world to me if you wore it. I'll buy you something—"

"Don't you dare. This is perfect. I'm not a jewelry wearer, I don't own much, and I can't tell you how honored it makes me feel to have this on my hand."

"It never entered my mind to give it to anyone else. It's always been yours. In my head. My heart."

"I'll take care of it. Of you. Of us."

"Is it weird that I want to fuck you while you wear nothing but my ring?"

The shift from sentimental to sexual has me laughing.

"I want to claim you with my ring on your finger. I just blew my load, and my dick is hard as a rock again."

We both glance down at his cock where it stands from between his legs. "That looks painful."

"It does ache." He shoots me a cocky grin. "And as my fiancée, it's your job to take away my pain."

"Oh, is it?" I reach over, draw a fingertip from the root of his shaft to the plump weeping head. "Any idea how I can do that?"

"I have a few."

"Care to pick one?"

"You pick." His gaze is locked on where my finger plays

with the bead of moisture oozing from the slit. "I don't care. I'll sit here and let you do what you're doing until I spray all over your hand if that's what you want."

"For a guy who just lost his virginity, you have a dirty mouth."

"Jeez, now I'm imagining your mouth on me."

"Done." I'm out of bed, shoving him backward until he's flat on the floor, me positioned between his spread thighs, and I don't wait. Don't tease him or go easy. I lick my lips as I lean over and take him in my mouth.

I guess it's a night for firsts. I've never sucked a guy off, never wanted to. Not even when I thought about Bran over the years did I imagine doing this.

I never imagined I'd enjoy it either.

But I'm loving the feel of him in my mouth, sliding across my tongue, stretching my lips wide when I take him as deep as I can without gagging.

"Blake. Babe. Shit. Fuck." His fingers tangle in my hair, tug and grip, the slight sting zipping through my blood and pulsing in my pussy. "Not. Gonna. Last. Can't. Feels...too. Good."

His stilted words have me doubling down, bobbing faster. I cup his balls in one hand, roll them with my fingers, and grip the base of his shaft with the other, squeeze in a pulsing rhythm.

The sounds he makes, the desperation lacing them, has me sucking hard, deeper, on each slide down. And when I feel him hit the back of my throat, I swallow.

"Fuck!" Come bursts into my mouth, flooding my tongue and his cock.

I can't contain it, can't swallow fast enough to keep it inside, and when he pulls free, when my mouth is no longer stuffed with him, his release dribbles down my chin.

"Fucking hell. I just came and the sight of you with your

lips red and my come on your face, has my dick twitching to get inside you again."

Swiping the back of my hand over my mouth, I grin. "Well, you do have years of abstaining to make up for."

"It has nothing to do with that. It's you, Blake." He jackknifes up and palms my face. "Only you."

BRANTON

Resting up on my elbow I stare down at the sleeping woman beside me.

For the second time in my life, I've woken up next to a woman.

This time I remember every second of last night.

And this morning.

There isn't one part of the last few hours I haven't rerun in my head multiple times since my eyes blinked open about thirty minutes ago.

I can't keep the smile off my face, and I don't care if it's a goofy grin either. It feels like one. Because I feel goofy. Giddy with excitement and anticipation.

I want to jump out of bed and wake Blake up. Drag her into the shower and turn another of my fantasies into reality.

Except I can't stop looking at her. At the ring on her finger. *My* ring.

"You're staring."

"I am."

"Why?"

"Because the sight of you next to me is one I've waited my whole life for."

"Jeez, you're going to be all mushy and lovey-dovey, aren't you?"

"Problem with that?"

She cracks open the eye closest to me. "Maybe."

"*Oh*." I frown. I don't know if I can curb my emotions when it comes to her. She's all I've ever wanted and now I have her...

A burst of laughter has Blake rocking on the bed beside me. "You should see your face."

My frown deepens and I grab her hip, keep her still. "You winding me up?"

"Well, I did enjoy undoing you last night...and this morning."

"Yeah?" Leaning over, I brush my lips over hers. "Want to see how wound up we can get in the shower?"

"Do we have time?"

"There's always time for us."

Palming my chest, she pushes. "No, there won't be, but we'll make time when we don't have a lot of it. What time is it anyway? Mom was planning a feast for breakfast."

"Her blueberry pancakes?"

"I expect so."

"Then why the hell are we dilly-dallying?" Tossing back the covers I roll out of bed.

"Dilly-dallying?" She giggles. "What kind of word is that?"

Shrugging, I bend down and scoop her up. "Don't know. I heard it somewhere."

"What are you doing?" Blake wraps her arms around my neck as I move toward the door.

"Getting in the shower."

"Together?"

"Yes. We're saving time and water."

"I'm not sure we'll save time."

"Oh, we will. We need to fuck and get ready. This way we can do them both at the same time."

"We need to fuck?"

"You don't agree?" I clear the bedroom doorway as well as the bathroom one without banging any of Blake's limbs—or head—on the way through. "Shit. You don't have any clean clothes down here."

"I can borrow something of yours to get from here to my room."

"No. Get in the shower, I'll race up and grab you something."

"You might run into my brothers. Or parents."

"Your parents are on the other side of the house, and I don't care if I bump into Landon or Corbin."

"We didn't talk about what happened last night when you found Landon."

"Later." I lower her to her feet and pat her ass. "Now get in the shower. I'll be back."

I do the smart thing and grab pants before I leave the suite of rooms that were my home from the time I was six.

I thought being here might be hard but when we arrived the other day I felt surrounded by love, had nothing but fond memories. I guess the other grief in my life outweighed any sadness I might have felt at being here without Mom.

The house is quiet and while it's not super early, it's not late either. I expect Andrew and Larissa are either still in their suite or the kitchen, and Landon may not have returned to the room he shares with Corbin at all.

As I make my way to the stairs, I hear noise coming from the corridor leading to the home gym and basement rinks. Voices and weights clanking. For a second I debate heading that way, seeing how things are this morning, but then I remember I have a naked Blake in my shower and there's no decision to be made.

Blake wins.

Will win every time.

Rushing up the stairs I'm in her room, rummaging in her duffel bag for a second before I think of a better option. Shouldering the bag, I duck into her bathroom to see if she has any toiletries laid out that she might need. Finding the counter bare, I shake my head.

Blake is so sexy she puts my body on edge, and yet she never does anything to emphasize her appeal. She's naturally gorgeous but doesn't flaunt it. I'm pretty sure she's oblivious to her looks.

I shouldn't compare her to the only other woman I've lived with but... Celeste had pots and tubes and bottles of all sorts of fragrant lotions and potions and not once did I find her sexy.

Another reason why waking in bed with her confused the fuck out of me. I'd never found any woman attractive enough to take to bed. Whether that was because I was already in love with Blake or not, I don't know.

Don't care.

I have the woman I've always wanted, she's wearing my ring, and I'm staring at an empty bathroom when she's naked in a different one.

"Jeez, you're a dumbass," I mutter as I spin around and leave the room.

I'm in the hall, almost to the stairs when a door behind me opens. Glancing over my shoulder I see Landon step out of the room. He looks rough. Like he hasn't slept at all. I stop and turn to face him.

"Hey."

My voice snaps his head up and halts him in his tracks. He gives me a forced smile. "Hey."

"You doing okay?"

"No. But I will be."

"If you need—"

"I know. I'll call."

"We don't have to talk about it. We can just get a beer, hang out, talk about hockey. Like we used to."

"Hmm..." His gaze lands on the bag slung over my shoulder and a grin tips his mouth up on one end. "Going somewhere?"

"No. Yes. Shit. I need..." I indicate the stairs.

"Don't fuck it up."

"I don't intend to. And if I do, I'll let you kick my ass."

"Won't need to. She'll kick it herself."

I grin. "Yeah, she will."

"When I get my head straight, I'll give you a call. Maybe come see where my sister is building this new team."

"You should. She'd love that. She'd love all of you to come see."

"We'll organize it. Maybe after the season. Before things really get moving for you guys at the Rogues."

"Sounds like a plan."

"Don't you need to..." Landon points behind me.

"Shit. Yes. Sorry. I left—"

Landon's hand shoots up. "Don't say it! I don't want that in my head."

Laughing I turn around and head for the stairs. "See you later."

I don't say when. He might show up to breakfast or he

might not. At this point we need—*I* need—to let Landon take the reins of our friendship. If we still have one.

I think we do. I hope we do.

Then again, I've managed to rebuild my relationship with Blake, with their parents, I'm sure I can salvage the remnants of mine and Landon's, Corbin too. I haven't a clue how Mason and Sutton feel about me. They're so much older that I was never that close with either of them. Even when we were younger and all living under this roof.

I guess if I'm going to marry Blake, and I am, no doubt about that, I'll need to make the effort with her two older brothers.

I should probably be the one to reach out first. Maybe I can ask Andrew for their numbers and get the ball rolling there. Possibly organize that trip for Blake's family to visit Baton Rouge after the season...

By the time I'm back in my rooms, my mind is spinning with all the ways I could handle her family and how we might keep a visit from them a secret from her. Except the second I enter the bathroom all thought is wiped cleaner than the ice behind a resurfacing machine.

Blake is naked, water running down the front of her, dripping from her pert nipples. She's leaning back against the tile wall, a hand between her legs...

Fuck.

She's my teenage fantasy come to life.

"Thought I'd have to finish without you."

"Yes." My dick throbs and I palm it through my pants. "Do that. Finish."

Her movements stop for a split second before the sexiest grin I've even seen curves her mouth. "This another teenage fantasy?"

"Fuck yes." I shove my pants to my knees and wrap a fist

around my pulsing shaft. "Dreamed of finding you in the shower. Of watching you get yourself off while I hid behind the door so you wouldn't see me do the same."

"No more dreaming."

"No." I squeeze my dick in an attempt to hold back my release. I don't want this to be over too fast.

"Want to join me in here or stay out there?"

I swallow. "If I join you, we won't get off like this."

"No?"

"No. I won't be able to control myself. I'll have to get inside you."

"Well, if you're serious about having a baby we shouldn't waste—"

She doesn't finish her sentence before I'm kicking my pants off and launching over the edge of the tub to join her in the shower. "Turn around."

My hands are on her hips helping her comply and I use my grip to bend her over.

"Hands on the wall. Hold on."

I don't give her a chance to argue, I step as close as I can, flex my knees, and line up my dick.

"Gonna fuck you raw so we can make our baby."

"Bran." She lets go of the wall with one hand, uses it to grab mine where it rests on her hip. "Your dirty mouth."

"I've had years and years to think about all the things I want to do to you. For so many of those I didn't think I'd get the chance." I buck my hips, press the head of my dick into her hot, slick heat. "Now that I can do them, can talk about them, I'm not going to stop."

With one thrust I'm balls deep and neither of us can speak. It's all moans and groans, whimpers and sighs, and panting breaths filling the room along with the steam from the shower.

We don't last long. The fiery edge of our need riding us

both in a fast gallop up and over, tossing us into simultaneous orgasms that have cries of pleasure echoing off the walls.

Breathing hard, plastered to the back of her, I press my lips to her bare shoulder, nudge the side of her neck with my nose. "I love you."

"I love you too."

Blake

Landon has shut down. He's here but not. Going through the motions of spending time with us.

No one pushes him. But Corbin is never far from his side and Bran seems to gravitate close too.

"He's not going to be ready before they leave."

I glance at Mom. "What?"

"Landon. He won't be ready to talk about Laura before tonight when they have to go back to New York."

"No. He won't."

"Will Branton be okay with that?"

"Yes. They talked. Landon asked for time to process, Bran's giving it to him. If anyone knows time is needed to deal with this, it's Bran."

"True." She taps my left hand. "Want to tell us about that? Maybe give us all something to focus on other than…"

"Ah, sure. We aren't really hiding it. But I think Bran wanted to talk to Dad first."

"Even though he already put a ring on your finger?"

"Yes." Bran slips an arm around my waist. "The ring is a

sign of my seriousness. And I don't need either of you to give me permission to marry Blake, that's hers to give, but I would like your blessing."

"You have mine. I think Andrew is in his office. Said something about preparing for negotiations with an agent," Mom says with a smile at Bran. "I believe the agent he's referring to is yours?"

"Ah, yeah, with everything I totally forgot about that."

"Well, why don't you go deal with that"—Mom raises my hand to highlight my ring—"and this. Blake and I will get brunch set up on the patio. It's a nice morning to eat outside."

"How long do I have?" Bran asks.

"Let's say fifteen minutes."

"See you then." Bran gives me a side hug and drops a kiss to my forehead before letting go.

I don't see him walk away because my gaze is on Landon.

My brother is standing in front of the wall of photos Mom continues to add to. From the time Mason was a baby until now, every few months there's a new picture on display.

The sadness on my brother's face makes me want to hold him. "I'll just go talk to Lan—"

"Nope." Mom grips my hand. "You'll help me get brunch on the table."

"But—"

"You can't fix this for him—them. No more than I can. And I'm the mom. My need to fix anything wrong for you kids is next level and as much as I want to go over there and talk to him, I'm not going to. He'll come to me when he needs, if he needs, and I'll have to be happy with that."

"Oh."

"He'll go to Corbin first. Then your dad. Bran for information the other two can't give him."

"I can't stand to see him hurting."

"Wait until it's your child hurting. You'll be crawling out of your skin."

Slipping an arm around Mom's shoulders, I lean my head on hers. "I'm here if you want to talk."

"Thank you. But your dad's pretty good at listening and you need to concentrate on you and Branton." She grins at me. "And a wedding."

My gaze find hers. I want to see her reaction to what I say next. "Bran wants to get married sooner than later. He wants to start a family too."

"What do you want?"

"The same as him. We've waited a long time to get to this point." I glance down at my hand, at the ring. "It's his mother's ring."

"I thought I recognized it."

"I was beginning to think getting married and being a mom might not be in the cards for me."

"You're not that old."

"No. But I never thought about marrying anyone else, being a mother to anyone else's children. Even when I thought he was in love with another woman and having a baby with her, finding someone else to do those things with never crossed my mind."

"Well, as much as I've pressed for years for more grand babies, I know I'm—*we're*—lucky to have Cash. Emma could have not told us about him. Any more in our future will be a blessing."

"I'm sorry her and Mason didn't stay together."

"I'm old, not stupid," Mom laughs. "I know they were never together as a couple."

I cringe. "Sorry. I like to think of it like that because the idea of my brother hopping from bed to bed…" I shudder.

"I know. I'm his mother, it's ten times worse." Laughing

she tugs me toward the kitchen. "Now help me get this food outside."

"I need to research what we have to do to get married here."

Mom's gaze snaps to mine. "Here? As in *here*, here? This house?"

"Oh, no. Well, maybe." I shrug. "I don't know. Bran wants to get married as soon as we can, and my only request is we do it in Canada. Can we do it here at the house? Where we met and fell in love?"

"Did you fall in love here?"

"Ah, me, no. But Bran did. And I think it would be a nice way to circle back to us. Make our union official in the place we've spent a lot of time together. Plus, this is the last place he was close to his mom."

"All right. We'll get brunch set out, then you and I will get on my laptop and see what we can find out."

"You'd let us get married here?"

"Of course. Why wouldn't we?"

"I don't know. I never thought about it until you mentioned it and I'm wondering if maybe we should wait, do something bigger where everyone has time to travel, to get here, and Dad can give me away."

"What do you want?"

"Something small. I liked what Oakley and Walker did. It was just the two of them, Pa and Micky and the officiant. The officiant's wife as a second witness."

"Okay, then you'll have that. Or your version of it."

"Down by the pond?"

"You don't want it somewhere... Never mind. Down by the pond would be perfect for you both."

"Is it still frozen? Maybe we could get married in our skates."

"You want...?" Mom shakes her head. "Of course you do."

"It's fitting, right? We spent a lot of time out there skating."

"And if not out there, you were in the basement."

"Now that I think about it, we could do it downstairs on the rink. No worries about the pond still being frozen."

"No. Your father keeps the basement frozen twenty-four-seven-three-sixty-five."

"He only defrosts it once every four years?"

"What? No, he leaves—" I duck, Mom's hand barely skimming to top of my head. "Smart ass."

Laughing, I dance away. "Sorry. Couldn't resist."

"Here." She opens the oven door and pulls out a tray filled with blueberry pancakes. "Take these out to the table, put them in the warmer."

"Bran and the twins will demolish these in seconds. What are the rest of us eating?" I take the pan, the metal slightly warm against my skin.

"I've got another couple of trays in here. Bacon. Cinnamon rolls. Those mini egg muffin things I used to make you all for your early morning rides to the rink."

"You're spoiling us."

"As is my right."

"I'll take these out then go round up everyone while you get whatever else you've got prepared on the table."

"Take that tray then find the twins, send them in here to help. I'll give Bran another few minutes with your father before I rope them into helping too."

Light flashed on my hand catching my eye. "Should I take off my ring?"

"No. Don't you dare hide your excitement because of what's happening with your brother."

"I just thought it might not be the best time—"

"It's the perfect time. It'll give him something else to focus on."

"Oh. You're right. And that gets me thinking."

"Always a dangerous thing. Last time something got you thinking, you ended up owning an NHL team."

"Ha! True. But haha. How do you think Mason and Sutton would feel if Bran and I got married with the twins here and not them?"

"What exactly are you thinking?"

"Well, you said it would give Landon something else to focus on and I thought maybe I could ask him to stand up for me and Corbin to stand up for Bran."

"You don't want to get married as soon as you can then?"

"No, I still want that."

"The twins leave at seven tonight. When did you think you could slide in a wedding between now and then? Not to mention we don't know if you have to wait or can get married the day you apply or get a license or register or whatever it is you need to do."

"You don't remember?"

"Honey, I hate to break it to you, but your dad and I had a shotgun wedding in Vegas."

"You did not! You had that beautiful ceremony in the park where you met."

"Yes, we did have that, but it was all for show, not a legal wedding. And that was *after* Mason was born. Our first anniversary to be exact."

"Why do I not know this?"

"Because your grandmother was ashamed of us getting pregnant out of wedlock and to appease her, we never talked about our real wedding. Besides, we have no pictures of our official day except one with Elvis Presley and Dolly Parton."

"You got married in Vegas by Elvis and Dolly?"

"Yep."

"Oh my god! I have to see that picture."

"You have. It's in your dad's office. On the bookshelf behind his desk."

"I thought that was when you went to Vegas for Uncle Dan's wedding."

"No. He might have gotten married in Vegas but he didn't do it in an off the strip chapel with celebrity impersonators. His wedding was a huge flashy affair at the Bellagio. And it was six years after us."

Shaking my head I walk toward the glass doors to the patio. "I can't believe I've never known any of this."

"Let's get brunch on the table and everyone's plates filled then I'll tell you how your grandmother forced your father to make an honest woman out of me with a pitchfork."

I almost trip over as I step outside. "A what?"

"A pitchfork. You're going to love this story."

"Sounds like it."

BRANTON

"We can get married today?"

"You said you wanted to as soon as possible."

"I did, I do. I'm just shocked that it can happen that fast."

"We just need to apply for a license. Once we have that, it can be used any time in the next ninety days."

"And we can get a license today?"

"Yes. If we hurry. Mom knows someone who works in the municipal offices and can get us in on the quiet this afternoon to apply. Or tomorrow. Up to us."

"What are you thinking?"

"I thought if we got it today, we could maybe have Landon and Corbin as our witnesses."

"Who would officiate?"

Grinning, Blake says, "Mom knows someone who can do it."

"Of course she does." I look at my watch. It's just after noon. "Okay, let's do it."

"Dad will drive us to get the license and Mom will stay here to get everything else organized so we can have the ceremony before the twins need to leave to go back to New York."

"Wait. We're getting married *here*!"

"Ah, yeah. What did you think I meant?" Concern wrinkles her brow.

"To be honest, I don't know. That we'd go somewhere maybe."

"I thought it would be nice to have it somewhere we've spent a lot of time together. Down on the pond or on the rink downstairs..."

Slowly my mouth curls into a smile. "In our skates?"

"Fitting for us, don't you think?"

Pulling her close, I lower my forehead to rest on hers. "You undo me."

"Is that a good thing?"

"It's the very best thing." Dropping a quick kiss on her lips I pull back and grab her hand. "Let's go. We have a license to get."

"Hang on. We need our IDs for the application."

"Anything else?" I ask as I turn, tug her toward my room where our luggage is.

"No. Just two forms of ID."

"Passport and driver's license?"

"Yes, those will work."

I might have cut myself off from the world, but I kept things up to date. Thankfully.

It takes us a few minutes to collect what we need and check everything is valid. I knew mine were and I assumed Blake's were too, but I want all our i's dotted and t's crossed before we leave the house. I want no delays.

"Where's your dad?"

"Waiting in his office. Mom's in there making some calls.

She wants us to have a nice setup even if we insist on getting married on ice."

"Like what?" I don't need any fancy decorations. All I need is to say my vows and hear Blake say hers.

"Flowers I think." Glancing over my shoulder I see her shrug. "She'll probably put some sort of carpet on the ice too."

"She still won't go on it?"

"No. Slipping while pregnant with the twins really spooked her. As far as I know she hasn't been on it, with or without skates since."

"That's a shame. She was good."

"She was. Dad still tries to get her out on the pond every Christmas. But she never does, won't even let him carry her out there."

"Hmm..."

As long as I've known Larissa Watts, she's never walked on the ice without something laid over it. Cardboard, carpet, plywood sheeting. Doesn't matter what it is as long as it's not bare ice. And I only know she can skate because of all the home videos Andrew has shown us over the years.

The year Mason signed his first NHL contract, he wanted to commemorate the occasion with photos on the pond. We had to pull a sled with Larissa on it out to the middle because she refused to take part any other way.

"She can do whatever she wants for her to feel okay joining us."

"You don't mind having them there? At the ceremony?"

"C'mon. Talk while we walk." I slip my hand in hers and pull her close. "And just so we're clear, all I want to do is get married to you. I don't care who is or isn't there to watch it happen."

"Are we going?"

We both turn to find Andrew in the doorway of his office.

"Yes." "Yes."

Looking back at Blake, I grin. We've been doing that more each day. It seems the longer we spend together, the more in sync we become.

"Then let's get out of here. Your mom has a list of things as long as my arm she wants me to pick up while you two deal with the paperwork. I've also been given strict instructions to drop you off in the underground garage near the staff entrance where Maggie will meet us. She'll usher you into the building with as little exposure as possible."

"She thinks we need the secrecy?" I follow Andrew through the house. "Surely there won't be any reporters waiting around in case they spot someone worth printing about in the media."

"Now days it isn't about reporters or photographers getting the scoop. It's the public with their smart phones and social media. One pic, a few words of where you were spotted, and it'll be all over the internet before the ink is dry on your license and the place will be swarming with fans and media."

"Ah, true. I forgot how exposed social media has made everyday life." I shouldn't have. It's how the story of my marriage to Celeste broke. It's how the news of Laura's death was revealed to the world.

Blake's hand squeezes mine. "It's fine. We'll keep our jackets and tuques on. Keep our heads down. I'd say we should wear sunglasses but that would be like a red flag to a bull."

"Definitely no glasses. And after the ceremony you two can choose which pictures you want to share with the world and post them yourselves. Or let me or one of your brothers post."

"I'll call Cami when we get back. Get some ideas, put together a plan so we beat them, whoever they are, to the punch."

"Do you want them here? Cami and Oakley? Nat?" I know

we're rushing. I'm rushing. Except now that we're here, with my ring on her finger, heading out to get a marriage license, I don't want to slow down.

"No. We'll video call with them, Mason and Sutton too. Mom said she'd organize it."

"As long as you're okay with doing it, getting married this way."

"Bran, I just want to get married. It doesn't matter to me how we do it. I told you, my only request is doing it in Canada."

Smiling down at her I'm struck by how quickly things have changed. How much *I've* changed. "I can't believe I get to call you wife by the end of the day."

"Believe it."

Andrew's phone beeps, drawing our attention. Looking at it he scowls. "Damn woman. Can't I at least get out of the house before you give me more things to do?" he grumbles while tapping on the screen.

"Is that Mom?" Blake grins, obviously knowing the answer.

"Yes. I have another list of things to get." Glancing up he says, "You two be okay if I leave you at the municipal offices while I go pick up everything your mom thinks we need?"

"Of course."

"You should be fine. It'll take a bit to get the paperwork filled out and approved, although Maggie said she'll put a rush on it, walk it through the process to make sure it doesn't sit waiting on anyone's desk." He looks at his phone again. "It should only take me an hour or so to get everything on Mom's list."

"All right. Let's get going. The quicker we get there, the quicker we get back." Blake leads the way to the attached garage, her hand gripping mine tight, not that I'm letting go or going anywhere she isn't.

Andrew slaps my shoulder. "Best learn to follow the wife. Smartest thing you'll ever do."

"I would think the smartest thing is convincing her to be my wife in the first place."

BLAKE

Never once have I thought about what my wedding would be like. I was never one of those girls dreaming of their Prince Charming and the perfect wedding. No time for any of that when my biggest concern was beating my brothers and Bran on the ice.

Getting married, having kids, was always an abstract thought. I knew it would happen at some point in the future. It was the man that was crystal clear. But even then, I was mid-twenties before those thoughts solidified, before I knew who it would be.

Now here I am. Standing in a pair of skates I haven't worn in years, my hands gripping Bran's, in the basement of my parents' house, my brothers and friends looking on.

And it's perfect.

I don't know how Mom did it. How she got this gorgeous setting put together on such short notice.

There are small potted trees lining the rink, the same ones that edge the pond out back. We're standing beneath an arched trellis of climbing roses, as well as pots of colorful mixed flowers lining the aisle I just skated down with Dad and spread out around the two sections of white carpet everyone is congregated on.

If I didn't know there was roof over my head, I'd think I was outside.

She's turned this cold, artificially lit basement rink into an outdoor wonderland.

Our plan to marry on the pond got washed out by the storm that rolled in while we were in town applying for our license.

I'd been so disappointed on the drive home, my dad's words of reassurance doing nothing to lift my mood. Then I walked through the front door to find *all* my brothers at the house. I knew Landon and Corbin were here, but the sight of Mason and Sutton had tears streaming down my face.

Four hours later, minutes before Dad was to skate me down the aisle, Oakley, Cami, Nat, and Walker came through the front door.

Their arrival prompted excited chatter and a round of hugs and more tears, but the slightly red, puffy eyes that are sure to show in my wedding pictures are worth it to have them at my wedding.

Everyone who's important to me is here. Even Cash. How Mason got him from Emma in enough time to make the drive up from Toronto I don't know but I'm grateful.

Almost as much as I'm grateful for being here. For finding my way back to Bran. Or him finding his way back to me.

It doesn't matter who found who. We're where we should be.

Where we should have always been.

"Welcome. Thank you for joining me in celebrating the love Blake and Branton have for each other. They are thrilled you were able to join them at such short notice on this special day to witness them take this next step, to see them join their lives from this day forward."

I glance at Callum. I've known him my entire life; he's been one of my parents' closest friends since before I was born, and I had no idea he could legally perform marriages.

When he arrived, he sat us down and asked what we would like to do in the way of vows. Having talked about that very thing while waiting for our license, we knew we wanted to say our own, that we wanted to speak from our hearts more than have him repeat something generic he's used multiple times in the past, so we asked him to keep his words simple, quick.

"Branton, do you take Blake as your lawfully wedded wife?"

"I do." Bran's words are clear, strong, and the smile on his face has mine growing to match.

"Blake, do you take Branton as your lawfully wedded husband?"

"I do."

"I believe you both have some words you would like to say to each other."

"Yes." "Yes."

I grin at Bran, and he squeezes my hands, holds them tighter.

"Bran, would you like to go first?"

"Yes. Thank you."

With another squeeze of my hands and a deep breath, Bran begins.

"Blake. You are, have always been the light in my days, the star that lights my nights. Without you, my life is dark, bleak, not a life at all, and I will spend every minute I have left on this planet earning my place in your light. I can never thank you for what you give me, what you will give me for the rest of my days. I can only offer myself, my heart and soul, my devotion, and with each breath I take, I'll strive to be the best man I can be for you. Because my heart beats for you. Has always beat for you. Only you."

My eyes well with tears and I have to swallow hard, blink several times, before I can see him clearly again.

"Blake, when you're ready," Callum murmurs.

Clearing my throat, I grip Bran's hands like the lifeline he is, my gaze locked on his. "You are so many things to me. Have been so many things to me all my life, little brothers' best friend, competitor, friend, best friend, but the one I cherish the most is this one. Husband. I'm honored that you want to walk this life with me. Want to build a family with me. And with each step we take I want you to know I'll love you more with everything we do, everywhere we go. With every day, every minute, every second, I will love you a little deeper, a little harder. Because not loving you isn't an option. As long as there is breath in my lungs, a beat in my heart, I will love you, Branton."

I can hear a few sniffles behind me, and I know Mom hasn't bothered to find privacy for her tears today. Not these ones. Because these are happy tears. Just like the ones sliding down my own cheeks.

"It's my great pleasure to declare Branton and Blake, husband and wife."

Bran palms my face, his thumbs brushing through the dampness on my cheeks before he leans forward and follows each swipe with his lips.

"I love you." The words are whispered on my skin. "I love you."

Smiling, I grab the front of his shirt and pull him closer. "I love you too."

Our kiss is quick. Nothing like the ones we've shared up

until now. This kiss is soft and sweet and full of the reverence we both feel for what we've just done.

Less than two weeks ago I hadn't seen, hadn't spoken, to Bran in years. And now, I have his ring on my finger, he has mine on his, and what I said is true. I will love him more with every breath I take because every beat of my heart whispers his name in my chest, has since I was twenty-five, and as we face our family and friends, I make a silent vow to never let either of us lose sight of our love.

No matter what the world throws at us, no matter who tries to get in our way, we will never forget the way we feel ever again.

BRANTON

Wife.

The word holds so much emotion. A thin trace of resentment underscores the pleasure, the rightness of having a wife.

I know I shouldn't let thoughts of the past intrude on today but it's hard to keep them out. Especially when Landon looks at me like I kicked his puppy.

The only consolation I have is Mason Watts has gone out of his way to apologize to me for all the 'bad things' he's thought and said about me in recent years.

I wasn't shocked when he cornered me to talk. More shocked when he told me Landon had confided in him about our situation. That he's here for me if I need someone to talk to. I've never had that from Mason before but I'm relieved. Happy he's looking at our marriage favorably.

Sutton has also been appraised of the situation with Laura, another shock, although I do know Landon and Corbin have always had close relationships with all of their siblings.

The subject of Laura has been a hushed murmur between

myself and all the Watts throughout the day. The only one I haven't spoken to about it is Landon.

Mason thinks in spite of Landon disappearing after the ceremony that he'll be okay, that he'll come around quickly.

I'm not so sure.

We haven't seen him since he left a couple of hours ago and now it's time for him and Corbin to fly back to New York.

I know Corbin is worried; we all are, but in my experience, it doesn't matter how concerned those around you are. You need to find your way through on your own.

Corbin did mention he caught Landon on the phone with the woman he's been seeing a couple of times throughout the day. And I'm hopeful she can help him navigate this emotional upheaval.

I'll be here waiting when he makes it through, when the time comes for me to help him find answers or wants to know about Laura.

"Why are you looking so serious, husband? What are you thinking about?"

Grinning at Blake, I wrap an arm around her and yank her against me. "The usual shit, *wife*."

"It's weirdly right to call each other that, isn't it?"

"Yes."

"I know it's not the time, but I still think Mom's suggestion to find a grief counselor is a good one. The right one."

"We can look into it when we get home."

"Home?"

"Baton Rouge."

Her eyes search mine and I know she's trying to decide if she should say something or not.

"Just say it."

"What about your house in New York? The things you said you have in storage?"

"I have no personal effects in the house, had it shut up, furniture covered before I left. I'll sell it as is. The contents of the storage locker I'll have shipped to Baton Rouge as soon as we're settled there. You can help me sort through it."

"You don't want to go back to the house?"

"No." I tap her temple with a finger. "I see your brain working. I don't need or want to see the house again. It was never my home, and I removed every personal item, everything of Laura's, I had there when I packed up to head north."

"If you want to take some time, on your own—"

Pressing my fingers to Blake's mouth, I smile. "Never on my own. I will never need you to step back for anything ever again. Things don't turn out right when I do them without you at my side. I don't intend to go it alone in the future, not even for a day."

"If you're sure." She's pensive for a moment. "I'd understand."

"You would but it's not necessary. I told you, you are my light, day and night. Without you I'm in a dark, depressing place. One I never want to see again."

"Okay, okay. I get it. And I hope you know I don't want to do anything without you either."

"Good. Because I have no intention of letting you."

Blake glances around before leaning in to whisper close to my ear. "Do you think they'd notice if we disappeared for the night?"

"I think if they did, they'd forgive us but don't you want to say goodbye to everyone? I thought they were all heading out tonight."

"Everyone except Mason and Cash. He said he needs to talk to Mom and Dad about something."

"Is something wrong? He seemed okay when we spoke earlier."

"I think it has to do with Cash. Or Cash's mom, Emma."

"I don't remember much about her, and Cash has grown so much since I saw him last." My eyes find him across the room. He's laughing at something Sutton is saying.

Blake follows my gaze and smiles. "Yeah, he shot up this past summer and with his voice starting to crack, he's no longer the little boy who used to follow us all over the place."

"No, he's not. What is he now, thirteen?"

"Fourteen last month."

"I guess we'll find out if we're supposed to. But enough about your brother and nephew, let's revisit the getting out of here comment. Why don't we do the rounds and say goodnight to everyone, ask your mom if she needs any help tidying up."

"I've got enough recruits for cleanup if you two want to call it a night."

Turning, we find Larissa has come up behind us, a glass of sparkling wine in hand, a smile on her face.

"Go on. Get out of here. I'll see you both in the morning."

"We should say goodbye."

Giving a shrill whistle, one I haven't heard since I was a teenager and Larissa used to stand on the back patio and whistle so we could hear her out at the pond, she gets everyone's attention. "Say goodnight to the newlyweds!"

A chorus of goodnights ring out and Blake and I are laughing when Oakley blows a bunch of bubbles over us. In seconds everyone else has joined in and we're leaving the living room in a shower of glittering bubbles.

And when we make it to my suite of rooms, to where fourteen-year-old me worked out what the way I felt about Blake meant, I take her hand and turn off the lights as I lead her to my room.

"I know the size isn't ideal and we should probably head up to your room, but I want our first night to be here, in my bed."

"Of course. Besides, if we haven't got much space, that just means we'll need to be closer."

Palming her face, I tip her head back and meet her gaze. "I love you. Thank you for forgiving me. For letting me love you in the open."

"There was nothing to forgive. I never really thought there was. I only wish I could have been there to love you through your darkest days."

"You were." I place a hand on my chest. "In here. You were always in here. Will always be in here."

"I want to take your name."

I bring my hand up and cover her lips. "No. Well, yes. But I have something else in mind, something I spoke to your mom and dad about earlier."

When she tilts her head, her gaze urging me on, I explain.

"I think we should take each other's last names. The same as Laura. Blake Cary Lattimer Watts and Branton Davis Lattimer Watts."

"Oh, Bran." Her eyes fill. "It's perfect."

"It feels right. Your parents agreed, thought it would be the perfect way to join us all together. When we get home, we'll work out how to make it happen."

"Before you sign the contracts."

"What?"

"We need to do it before you sign with Drake or the Rogues. Today is the first real day of your new life. And Branton Davis Lattimer Watts has one hell of a bright future to look forward to."

"He does. But before that..." Lifting her up, I toss her over my shoulder. "He's got a wedding night to get to."

PUCK BUNNY PROMOTIONS

UP TO DATE BUNNY TO WIFE
ANNOUNCEMENTS

Well, hockey fans, do we have a scoop for you today. Word on the street is that female hockey phenomenon Blake Watts has not only scored herself a team in the NHL, but she's also hooked herself a hot shot, for the Baton Rouge Rogues AND herself.

Branton Lattimer has finally come out of hiding and will be hitting the ice again soon. This time for the Rogues. And that's not all. Our source informs us that his name on the Rogues roster will read Branton Lattimer Watts.

And, bunnies, if you're savvy and keeping up with all the gossip about this shiny new NHL team for promotion potential, you might have seen the Rogues coaching staff list got some updates too. Blake Lattimer Watts is listed as assistant coach.

We have no confirmation from either Blake, Branton, or the Rogues, but you can rest assured that we will be doing our best to find out the details of what looks like a secret marriage. The second for Lattimer.

Hopefully this one won't end as tragically as the first.

BLAKE

We're barely in Baton Rouge a full day when the first article comes out.

On *Puck Bunny Promotions* of all places.

Fuck, I really hate that blog.

At least I can be grateful they didn't refer to me as a puck bunny. I'll take the hockey phenomenon title with a smile.

And if I'm honest, the post isn't that bad. I can do without the reference to Bran's first marriage but it's not like I can wipe it from existence even if that's what we'd both prefer.

"Hey."

Glancing up from my computer I find my husband—I love thinking of Bran as that—leaning on the doorframe. "Hey. Heading down to the ice?"

"Yes. Walker is going to do some work with me but I wondered if you had time to join us."

"I will in about twenty minutes."

"Meeting?"

"Video call with the man I'm hoping will captain the Rogues, and his agent."

"Oh?" Bran pushes off the doorway and comes toward me. "Anyone I know?"

"Probably."

"Care to share?"

He's grinning at me. We've been doing this dance for the last week. I've shared some names but not others. This one I'm okay with telling him.

"Beckett Higgison."

"Beck?" Bran tips his head toward the ceiling, a thoughtful look on his face. He's talking again before returning his gaze to mine. "He's a solid guy. Been around more than a few years, played only on Canadian teams but he's American, probably close to retirement so I'm not sure if he's a long-term strategy prospect. Keeps to himself off the ice, almost recluse-like. Might not fit in with the family atmosphere you want to build here."

I love how deeply Bran thinks about the players I tell him about. And his insights are always spot on. Smiling, I say, "You nailed what I know about it. And I think he will fit here. We need some solid, experienced players to round out all the young guys we're looking at bringing on. But I'm not the only one with a say and I have to feel out him and his agent, gauge their interest, before I can make an offer anyway."

"All right. I'll leave you to it." Planting his hands on my desk, he leans over and drops a kiss on my forehead. "See you on the ice."

"See you—*Oh!* Wait! I need to show you this." Clicking on the browser tab where the blog post about us is still up, I turn my monitor so Bran can read it. "*Puck Bunny Promotions* has us in today's post."

"Yeah, Nat messaged me about it a few minutes ago. Nothing bad though, right?"

"You didn't read it yet?"

"No. I figured Nat was on top of it and if not her, you would be." He shrugs. "I told you, I'm here to be your husband and play hockey. But if the latter messes with the former, I'm breaking contract."

"It won't, but I'm grateful for your dedication to us over your career. Even if I think it's misplaced."

"It's not. I did it for too long already and look what happened. I'm not taking any chances with us, Blake. Not ever again." He waves a hand at the screen. "And if this isn't a problem for you, it isn't for me."

"I won't let you toss your career away."

"I don't intend to, but I will not let it interfere with us. *Ever.*"

"Have I told you I love you today?"

"Yes. But not in the last few minutes so go ahead," he prompts with a grin and wave of his hand.

"I love you." Rising, I lean in for a kiss then press a hand to his chest and shove. "Now go. Get out on the ice and don't let Walker run you into the ground."

"I think he's looking forward to being out there. Especially now I know about his vision impairment. Being aware means I can give him a good one-on-one game."

"Don't go soft on him. He'll hate that."

"I won't. But I also won't take advantage of what is a disadvantage for him."

My alarm goes off, the two-minute warning I set myself for the call with Beckett Higgison and his agent, Mal Gordon, Bran's old agent. "Get. I need to get settled before this call."

"Love you," Bran says with a final kiss.

Sitting back in my chair, I watch his fine ass walk across my office. Smiling when he turns and winks at me before shutting the door.

Two weeks ago I sat in this chair waiting for another video

call about a hot shot. And I had no idea I'd be a married woman the next time I stepped inside this room.

Or that I would have secured that hot shot not only for the Rogues but for me.

OFF THE ICE
INSIDE THE PRIVATE LIVES OF YOUR FAVORITE
NHL PLAYERS

A name we haven't mentioned here on Off the Ice in quite some time is Branton Lattimer. And we're not even sure if this story refers to the same man as previous articles because it seems Branton Lattimer Watts is making appearances all over the hockey world right now.

First we heard rumors of agent Drake Morgan signing Branton as his newest client, then his name was touted as a possible starter for the new Baton Rouge Rogues NHL franchise.

And finally we can confirm, through Drake's office that yes, Branton Lattimer Watts is his newest client and has in fact signed a five-year deal to play for the Rogues.

But that's not all. We're also hearing the reason for the name change isn't a late in life adoption but a marriage. A marriage that just happens to be with his new assistant coach. Who, we note, has added Lattimer to her name. Blake Lattimer Watts, assistant coach and co-owner of the Baton Rouge Rogues, married Branton in a private ceremony at her parents' property just outside of Ottawa, Canada, last month. A property the newlyweds grew up on together.

We're not sure what's going on over at the Rogues camp. Mere weeks after the franchise announcement, we have co-owner Oakley James and newly appointed head coach, Walker Alcott, tying the knot. Now we have co-owner and assistant coach, Blake Watts, marrying newly signed hot shot Branton Lattimer.

Is it something in the water down there?

Should we keep an eye out for more nuptials as the Rogues roster fills up?

One thing is for sure—this new NHL franchise is stirring things up in the league. And they're doing it off the ice before they even lace up their skates.

EPILOGUE

BRANTON

I skim the article on *Off the Ice* and decide it's okay. I know Blake thinks I'm not concerned by what is printed about us, and I'm not as long as there's nothing objectionable said about my wife.

I don't give a fuck what they say about me, but my wife? Yeah, that's a death sentence to any journalist, gossip columnist, or social media influencer.

Not that the latter is too much of an issue but if the fans pick up on something, it will be.

When Nat warned us all she was getting the Rogues website updated with the latest additions, and that included front-end office staff, we waited with bated breath to see who might notice the changes.

So far it's been two of the more popular hockey blog sites and that's it.

Drake wants to do a press release.

Nat wants to wait.

Blake wants to shout it from the rooftop.

I'm happy to do the last.

In fact, I've got just that planned for tonight. I got the okay from Nat and Oakley, and surprisingly Cami came through for me too by getting everything I need and helping me set it all up.

Tonight, I'm going to take care of my wife because I know today was a long one for her. A tough one.

For all of them really, but I'm only concerned with Blake.

I thought about taking her home and running her a hot bath, but I know she hasn't done her usual celebration for me signing on as a Rogue. The last four weeks have been busy with negotiations with agents and players and handling the mudslinging some of the media are engaging in.

Everyone could do with a break and what better way than shouting good things from the rooftops?

I invited the others to join us up here to celebrate a couple of Rogues milestones they haven't been able to yet. Hopefully they can relax and enjoy the balmy spring night away from prying eyes and photographers' lenses.

Hearing voices echoing up the stairwell, I switch my phone off and tuck it away in the bag at my feet.

They're laughing and chattering, multiple conversations happening at once, and I smile.

I have no idea how they don't miss half of what's said but they're so in sync with each other, have known and worked together so long, it's like they share a brain at times.

I've barely witnessed it. But what I have seen explains why they're such a success. Even with Cami taking a back seat to the other three, the four of them speak a language all their own.

Walker's deep tones mingle with the lighter ones and I'm glad he got my message and decided to join us. I'm hoping he's got Micky with him.

I understand that little boy on a level I didn't comprehend until Blake said something about me being in his shoes before.

She meant losing my father young. But unlike me, Micky doesn't have his mom to keep him grounded.

Walker and Oakley are doing their best for him, and I've already made it clear to them, and Blake, that I want to help them with that anyway I can.

Inviting him to take part in this little celebration is my attempt to include him in our family.

He's part of it through his adoption but I want him to feel it as well as know it.

It's what the Watts family gave me as a kid—hell, they're still giving it to me, and I want to pay that forward.

"Wow!" Micky bursts through the doorway, his gaze bouncing around all the lanterns Cami helped me spread out on the rooftop.

"What's this?" Blake's the only one in the dark. Everyone else knew what to expect when they headed up here.

"This is a belated celebration of the newest member of the Rogues and the newest member of our family. Micky?" I call out. He's already off checking out the food and drinks. "Come over here a sec."

When Micky stands beside me, his face, so much like Walker's tipped up to look at me, I get a longing so sharp and deep I have to suck in a breath.

"You know Blake, right?" He nods. "Well, she's done this thing to celebrate good things since she was little, like you are, and I think we should make it our thing too. What do you say, want to celebrate with us?"

"Is there cake?"

Laughing, I ruffle his hair. "Yes, there's cake but not yet. First Blake has to show us how to celebrate."

When I look up, Blake's eyes are on me, hers filled with tears, but the smile she gives me is all the sign I need to know I hit the mark with this idea.

"All right. Our first celebration is for Micky. Blake, you want to take the lead?"

Stepping over, she drops down to her knees and grabs Micky's hands. "Ever since I was a little girl, I would find the tallest place around and shout about the good things that happened. It didn't matter what it was as long as it was a good thing. I'd yell what it was or say it then yell." Her eyes dart up to meet mine briefly. "And I think what Bran wants us to celebrate is you being here, with us. Forever."

Micky looks confused and I get that at four he's probably too young to understand what's going on, but he'll get it one day. Plus I can see Oakley has her phone out, no doubt videoing another of Micky's milestones.

"Okay. You ready?" Blake asks.

Micky nods, his eyes moving to where Walker and Oakley are. "Can they do it too?"

"Of course. We're all going to do it." Holding out her hand, Blake grabs mine and gives me a quick squeeze before letting go and taking both of Micky's again. "On the count of three we're going to yell your name at the sky. One. Two. Three."

"Micky!"

Our timing is a little off but not much. And by the time the last syllable fades away Micky is grinning ear to ear and bouncing on his toes.

"That was fun. Can we do it again?"

"We sure can but this time we have to yell Branton. Because he's going to play for the Rogues. You want to count this time?"

"Yes. One, two, three. Branton!"

Micky's excitement has us laughing and shouting my name. It's not as loud as his and definitely not as in sync but I don't need it to be.

A small hand curls around mine and I look down to see Micky looking up. "We're Rogues now."

"We are." Crouching down, I put my hand on his shoulder and turn him to face me. "No one can ever take that away from us. From you."

"I'm going be a real one when I grow up."

"A real one?"

"Yes. On the ice. A hot spot like you."

Laughter follows Micky's words and I look around to find everyone's eyes on us. "Well, we better get to training you then. Starting tomorrow, come to work with Walker and we can get you set up."

Looking over his shoulder, he waits for Walker and Oakley to nod before turning back to me. "Okay, but..." he chews his bottom lip. Leaning forward he whispers, "I'm not very good yet."

Mimicking him, I whisper back, "Don't worry. I wasn't very good at your age either."

"So I can get better?"

Walker's hand lands on Micky's shoulder as he crouches beside us. "Yes, you can. You will. And when you're old enough, we'll get you in a Rogues jersey."

"I have a jersey. LeeLee gave it to me. It has my name on it."

Looking up I see Blake watching me closely. She knows there's more than my childhood that draws me to Micky.

I miss Laura. I miss being a dad and I barely got the chance to experience it. But if I'm lucky, luckier than I already am, I'll be a dad again soon.

We suspect Blake is pregnant. She hasn't done a test or anything, but in the six weeks since she turned up in Parry Sound, we haven't been apart and in the five weeks since we first had sex we haven't once used protection.

My gut tells me we hit the jackpot, but I'm letting her lead this like I've let her lead everything else in this new life of mine.

"Should I wear my jersey tomorrow?"

Micky's question pulls me away from Blake back to him. "Maybe LeeLee or Walker can get you a practice jersey?"

"LeeLee!" Micky is racing off toward Oakley before Walker or I can stop him.

"He's all about her, isn't he?" I ask, as I rise alongside my old friend who's proving to be a damn good new one even though the line between friend and coach is one we'll have to navigate when more players sign on with the Rogues.

"Yeah." Walker's gaze follows Micky and stays on him when Oakley bends down to get on Micky's level. "She's all about him too."

"We both got lucky, didn't we? Hit the jackpot when our lives changed in ways we never thought we would come back from."

"Yep. Now we just have to make sure we don't fuck it up."

"Don't worry. I have no intention of fucking it up and every intention of making sure those four women get what they want."

"And what's that?" Walker's gaze snags mine.

"A successful team. A place in the finals our first year. And their hands on the Cup sooner than later."

EPILOGUE
BLAKE

Bouncing on my toes I try to soothe the fussy baby strapped to my chest but he's having none of it.

He's a Daddy's boy.

Most of the time that's not a problem. Bran is a hands-on dad and never far from our son. I'm pretty sure he's changed more diapers than I have in the nine months of Drew's life.

Normally I would hand him off to Bran. I'm not at all upset my son seems to prefer his father to me.

When Drew lets out another squawk of protest, I give in and lower myself to a seat. A couple of quick snaps and both of us are free of the carrier he hates unless it's attached to his dad and he's sitting on the floor at my feet happily babbling away.

I have no idea what he's saying but I'd bet money on it being about his dad. He's probably telling me to go get him.

Normally I would, except right now, Dad is on the ice in the first pre-season game of the Rogues inaugural year playing in the NHL.

We're in the owners box. Oakley and Nat are talking in

hushed tones off to the side. My parents, Mason, Sutton, and Cash are all hovering near the glass, watching the game.

I'd decided to come up here with Drew instead of being down with my team and I'm just as agitated as my son.

"Go down there. Leave him with us. Micky will keep him occupied and your mom and dad are here."

I look up at a frowning Oakley. "No. I'm good."

"You are not." Nat grips my elbow and tugs me from my seat.

"Hey!"

"Don't hey me. Get your ass down there and do your job!"

"But—" I break off when I see my son has crawled over to his namesake and is now perched in Dad's lap happily clapping his hands and babbling. "Shit. You're right. He's probably been fussy because I'm feeling out of sorts."

"Then get out of here so you can both feel better." Oakley gives me a little push. "Tell Walker I'll meet him before the press conference."

"Okay. See you downstairs later." I head over to Mom and Dad so I can kiss my boy and tell them where I'm going so I get to see my hot shot in action.

Everyone is on their feet when Beckett Higgison gets a clear shot to Bran who's got himself an even clearer path to the back of the net.

The arena comes alive with a roar. Every fan on their feet as the first goal of the game comes off a Rogues stick.

"Holy shit. That boy is on fire." Dad looks back at me. "I never said it before, but I was worried. I wasn't sure he still had it in him, not after…"

"I know. I get it. The media have been all over it since he signed with us."

"You heading down there?" Mason asks.

"Yeah."

"Can I bring Cash down later?"

"Of course." I glance at my nephew. He's doing okay but I've got something I want to run by my brother after the game and if he brings Cash down I can entice both of them to accept my proposal. "I'll get Oakley to give everyone passes."

"We have them. Just didn't want to presume."

"Presume away. If you've got a pass, use it."

"Thanks."

"See you later."

I duck out of the suite, hit the stairwell instead of the elevator because I need to work off some of this nervous energy.

It takes me no more than five minutes to get to the coaching staff's offices, then a short stroll to the change room and tunnel. It isn't until I'm almost out in the arena that I remember I removed my jacket up in the suite.

"Shit."

Spinning around I find Trevor, Oakley's former assistant turned Rogues fixer. "You might need this."

"Oh my god! You're a magician." Snatching the jacket from his hand, I slide my arms into the sleeves. "How did you know—"

"Please. I've been following you around picking up clothing since you had the next generation of Rogues." Shaking his head, he says, "Not even out of diapers and he already knows how to get a woman out of her clothes."

"Hey! That's not—"

"Joking!" He reaches out, straightens my collar, tugs the sides into place. "I won't say I told you so, but I told you so. Now get out there with your team."

Trevor grips my shoulders, spins me around, and pushes me forward. "What is it with people pushing me around today?" I huff.

"We're just making sure you are where you should be. And that's standing behind the bench yelling at your team for doing dumb shit with the puck."

I laugh. Trevor is not a fan of hockey. I have no idea why he doesn't like it. Who doesn't like hockey? Not that he lets his aversion to the sport stop him from being the team's right hand. None of us would function without him. "Can you check—"

"Check the family suite and make sure all the partners and children are being looked after."

"How the hell did you know I was going to ask that?"

"Were you?"

"Well, yes, but—"

He puts up a hand. "You are the assistant coach of the Baton Rouge Rogues. Your job is to worry about the players. It's our job, mine mostly, to worry about their families. Now go! We're two minutes from the end of the first half."

"Period. It's the first *period*."

"I don't need to know about your female piping."

I'm still laughing when Trevor disappears from sight.

And surprisingly, the nerves from earlier are gone.

"Damn. He's good." Pulling my phone from my pocket I shoot him a thank you text and Oakley one to suggest we give him a raise.

His reply is *why aren't you already yelling at your players*, and Oakley's is *how much?*.

I grin. Owning the Rogues, training the team while having and raising a baby is hard work. There have been numerous sleepless nights, but every one of those hard minutes is worth it to be surrounded by the family we've built.

A roar echoes down the tunnel and I'm sprinting to the exit. As I clear the doorway, I see the replay on the big screen and hear the announcer's booming voice.

"Another hot shot from Lattimer Watts. He's on fire today. All those naysayers are eating crow right now."

Yes, he is on fire. But then he has been since the minute he decided to come out of hiding.

Want to know who's next to find their happy ever after in the *Hot as Puck* world? Read *Hot Damn* and discover the secret this single dad is hiding.

For what's coming next, latest releases, sales and more, join
Rhian's Royal Readers
http://www.rhiancahill.com/contact/newsletter/

If you enjoyed this book, please consider leaving a review. It only takes a few minutes and you'll be helping other readers find stories they'll enjoy, as well as supporting authors you love.

Acknowledgments

Thank you! I'm thrilled and humbled that you picked up Hot Shot and spent precious hours reading about Branton and Blake.

Their story was hard to write (for obvious reasons) and at times I wondered why the hell I wanted to write a hero with so much emotional damage.

Bran is tough, but even the toughest crumble when dealt one of life's most horrible blows. Thank you for taking the journey with him as he fought his way back from the darkness he'd fallen into.

I hope this book wasn't as hard to read as it was to write (I went through a few boxes of tissues between the first word and last) but if it was, I'm glad you stuck it out with Bran and Blake as they healed past wounds and found their way back to each other.

xoxo
Rhian

About Rhian Cahill

Rhian Cahill is the alter ego of a former stay-at-home mother of four. With motherly duties rapidly dwindling, Rhian is able to make use of the fertile imagination she used to keep herself sane for all those years of slavery. Years spent living overseas and visiting tropical climates have helped inspire some steamy stories.

Multi-published in erotic romance, paranormal romance, and contemporary romance, Rhian, with the help of Mr. Muse, spends her days and nights writing.

When not glued to the keyboard you'll find her, book or knitting in hand, avoiding any and all housework as much as possible.

For more on Rhian –

Website – http://www.rhiancahill.com/
Newsletter signup – http://www.rhiancahill.com/contact/newsletter/
FaceBook – https://www.facebook.com/RhianCahillAuthor
Instagram – http://instagram.com/rhiancahill/
BookBub – https://www.bookbub.com/authors/rhian-cahill
Goodreads – https://www.goodreads.com/rhian_cahill

OTHER TITLES BY RHIAN CAHILL

CONTEMPORARY ROMANCE

Hot as Puck

Hot Stuff

Hot Shot

Hot Damn

Hot Puck

Hot Hook

Hot Date

Love Beach

Summer With a Fake Date

Merry With a Scrooge

Spring Break With a Baby Daddy

Evergreen Lake

Jingle Balls

Winter Lake Series

Love Me Like You Do

Love The Way You Are

When You Love Someone

Let Me Love You

Wild Rush Of Love

Party Games Series

Truth Or Dare

Spin The Bottle

Pass The Parcel (novella)

Are You Game? Series

7 Minutes In Heaven

Catch'n'Kiss

Red Light, Green Light

Hearts Are Wild Series

No More Talking (novella)

Dare You To (novella)

Mad Love

Boys Of Summer

Bondi Beach Boys

Sand, Surf And Sunnie

Only You Series

All Of You

Holiday Romances

Christmas Wishes

New Year's Kisses

Valentine's Dates

Secret Santa

Frosty's Snowmen Series

A Touch Of Frost

A Kiss From Kringle

A Taste For Kandy

Hot and Bothered

Doing Logan

Shut Up And Kiss Me

PARANORMAL ROMANCE

Coyote Hunger Series

Coyote Home

Coyote Wild

Coyote Whispers

Coyote Law (novella)

Coyote Lies

For a full list of available books visit

http://www.rhiancahill.com/books/

For what's coming next, latest releases, sales and more, join

Rhian's Royal Readers

http://www.rhiancahill.com/contact/newsletter/